ERIN JOHNSON

A SCORE TO KETTLE

A MAGICAL TEA ROOM MYSTERY

GET YOUR FREE NOVELLA!

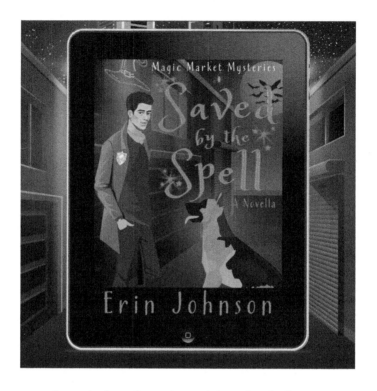

A magical academy. A suspicious death. Can an inexperienced cop expose the deadly secrets lurking behind bewitched classroom doors?

Download Saved by the Spell for FREE to solve a mystical murder today!

OTHER BOOKS BY ERIN JOHNSON

The Magical Tea Room Mysteries
Minnie Wells is working her marketing magic to save the coziest, vampire-owned tea room in Bath, England. But add in a string of murders, spells to learn, and a handsome Mr. Darcy-esque boss, and Minnie's cup runneth over with mischief and mayhem.

Spelling the Tea
With Scream and Sugar
A Score to Kettle
English After-Doom Tea

The Spells & Caramels Paranormal Cozy Mysteries
Imogen Banks is struggling to make it as a baker and a new witch on the mysterious and magical island of Bijou Mer. With a princely beau, a snarky baking flame and a baker's dozen of hilarious, misfit friends, she'll need all the help she can get when the murder mysteries start piling up.

Seashells, Spells & Caramels
Black Arts, Tarts & Gypsy Carts

Mermaid Fins, Winds & Rolling Pins
Cookie Dough, Snow & Wands Aglow
Full Moons, Dunes & Macaroons
Airships, Crypts & Chocolate Chips
Due East, Beasts & Campfire Feasts
Grimoires, Spas & Chocolate Straws
Eclairs, Scares & Haunted Home Repairs
Bat Wings, Rings & Apron Strings
* Christmas Short Story: Snowflakes, Cakes & Deadly Stakes

The Magic Market Paranormal Cozy Mysteries
*A curse stole one witch's powers, but gave her the ability to speak
with animals. Now Jolene helps a hunky police officer and his
sassy, lie-detecting canine solve paranormal mysteries.*

Pretty Little Fliers
Friday Night Bites
Game of Bones
Mouse of Cards
Pig Little Lies
Breaking Bat
The Squawking Dead
The Big Fang Theory

The Winter Witches of Holiday Haven
*Running a funeral home in the world's most merry of cities has its
downsides. For witch, Rudie Hollybrook, things can feel a little
isolating. But when a murder rocks the festive town, Rudie's
special skills might be the one thing that can help bring the killer
to justice!*

Cocoa Curses

Special Collections
The Spells & Caramels Boxset Books 1-3
Pet Psychic Mysteries Boxset Books 1-4
Pet Psychic Mysteries Boxset Books 5-8

Want to hang out with Erin and other magical mystery readers?
Come join Erin's VIP reader group on Facebook: **Erin's Bewitching Bevy.** It's a cauldron of fun!

ABOUT A SCORE TO KETTLE

Welcome to the coziest, vampire-owned tea room in Bath! It's steeped in magic and mystery.

You've got to have your bestie's back, right? Even if it involves stalking a vampire hunter?

Minnie Wells is getting back out there again after a messy divorce, when she attends a play at the gorgeous Theatre Royal in Bath with a hunky detective. But when Minnie finds the lead actress dead in her dressing room, her fun night out turns into a crime scene.

To heap on the trouble, Minnie also suspects her detective date's mysterious friend is the rumored vampire hunter.

Now Minnie's racing to solve the playhouse murder while protecting not only her best friend, but also her vampire boss (who she just might have a big crush on). All this, while working at the tea room, learning spells, celebrating the Spring Solstice, and dealing with her dastardly ex.

And it doesn't help when another body turns up backstage.

Will Minnie upstage the killer and keep her vampire friends safe? Or will it be curtains for this new witch and her paranormal pals?

Pull your armchair closer to the cozy crackling fire, sip your steaming tea, and find out now in *A Score to Kettle*!

If you like charming towns, a hilarious cast of lovable characters, and twisty mysteries, you'll adore Erin Johnson's lighthearted whodunnit. *A Score to Kettle* is the third book in the Magical Tea Room Mysteries.

Happy reading!

1

FINAL BOW

"The wishes, the hopes, the confidence, the predictions of the small band of true friends who witnessed the ceremony were fully answered in the perfect happiness of the union."

The deep, booming voice of the narrator trailed away, and the lights went dark. Heavy velvet curtains swished closed across the stage, and moments later the house lights lit up the theater. I glanced to my left and smiled at my date, DI Prescott—er, Clive. I was still getting used to calling him by his first name and seeing him without his partner, the older, gruff DI O'Brien. He looked quite handsome in his black blazer and khaki slacks.

I leaned over. "Did you enjoy the play?"

"Mm-hmm." He yawned and blinked, his eyes glassy. I grinned. He'd fallen asleep in the dark auditorium and woken with a jerk a couple of times.

The older couple to my right rose, and DI Prescott and I followed suit, along with the rest of the packed crowd, to give a standing ovation.

Although this was clearly not his thing, it'd been sweet

of Prescott to take me to see the play adaptation of Jane Austen's *Emma*. I'd mentioned my love of the author to him (though I hadn't let on to the full extent of my fangirling—I didn't want to scare him off). He'd remembered and planned the date around it—quite thoughtful of him.

Plus, despite having gone to university in Bath and having moved back several months ago now, I'd never actually been to the famous Theatre Royal before. It was a beautiful, historic building, and at first, I'd had a hard time paying attention to the play, the theater itself was so distracting. The plush velvet seats were comfortable and matched the burgundy-striped wallpaper that wrapped around the wall behind us. Prescott had gotten us great seats, right in the center of the highest balcony in the front. We had a great view of the stage, and the theater was small enough to be able to still read the actors' faces. High above our heads, an enormous, glittering chandelier bejeweled the carved plaster ceiling.

The man who'd narrated the play swept back on stage to enthusiastic applause and announced each of the actors by their names and the parts they played. One by one, they came out to thunderous applause and took their final bows.

"Bertram Kensington as Mr. Elton."

The plain-looking man pushed through the curtains, bowed, then stood beside the actress who'd played Emma's impressionable friend, Harriet.

"Elinor Barker as Jane Fairfax."

I clapped for the tall, elegant brunette who'd played Emma's rival-turned-friend.

"Harvey Smythe as Mr. Knightley."

The tall, broad-shouldered actor who'd played the dashing love interest bowed to enthusiastic applause.

"And finally..." The narrator swept his arms toward the

center part of the curtains. "Our star, Petra Cornflower as Emma Woodhouse."

The crowd erupted in raucous applause and whistles—by this time my palms stung. Petra swept onto the stage in her long skirts, her blond hair gathered into gorgeous curls atop her head. She dipped into a slightly wobbly curtsey, then beamed at the crowd. Suddenly, she frowned, scrunched up her face, and brought a gloved hand to her mouth as she sneezed, again and again.

I raised my brows. The handsome actor who'd played Mr. Knightley fished a kerchief from his coat pocket and handed it to her. She smiled, sniffled, then devolved into a sneezing fit again as she pressed the hankie to her red nose.

I winced. Poor girl. She'd been sneezing throughout the entire play. I'd bet she either had a cold coming on or a bad case of allergies. It was spring, after all, though in the cold climate of Bath, barely any plants had begun blooming.

The narrator, decked like the rest of the cast in Regency clothes that reminded me a lot of my vampire boss, Fitz, swept to the middle of the stage. He joined hands with the actors.

"Thank you all for attending this performance and for your support. If you wish to stick around, we'll be holding a meet the cast party out in the lobby, where you may also purchase refreshments."

They all folded into one last bow, their hands linked, and then the actors straightened and filed out behind the velvet curtain. The applause gradually died down, and then I turned with everyone else to gather my purse and program off my seat and wait my turn to file down the row and out to the lobby.

My date fell into step behind me, and I glanced over my

shoulder and smiled at him. "The meet the cast party sounds fun."

He smiled and nodded. "Sure."

I stifled a sigh and faced forward. Though it'd been fun and quite a unique experience, I couldn't help feeling a twinge of anxiety and disappointment.

Maybe it was because this was my first, first date in about seven years. My divorce from my ex, Desmond, was just about to be finalized, and I wasn't even sure I was ready to be dating again. Plus, it was so hard not to make comparisons. Not only to my ex, who'd not only failed to romance me while we were together, but who of late had accused me of hexing him (which of course, I hadn't). But also, and maybe more disturbingly, I found myself thinking of my boss, Fitz, who I happened to have a bit of a crush on.

Fitz and I could talk about deep, personal things with ease. I often worked on marketing from the kitchen of his tearoom, sitting on a stool across the worktop from him while he rolled bread dough or cut out scones. Our silences were comfortable, and our conversations flowed.

One of the ushers waved me towards the stairs, and I climbed down to the lobby. That wasn't quite fair to my date. I'd had more chances to talk to Fitz and get to know him, whereas pretty much all of my interactions with DI Prescott, aside from this evening, had occurred at crime scenes. Not exactly the most fertile ground for romance.

I just needed to give him more of a chance. We filed out into the noisy lobby where little circles formed around the actors.

"Care for a drink?"

I smiled at Prescott. "I'd kill for a glass of red." My smile faltered as I thought of the red liquid my vampire roommate

Gus often drank out of wineglasses—it certainly didn't come from any grapes.

Prescott took my hand and threaded through the crowd, gently pulling me behind him.

We passed the beautiful brunette who'd played Jane Fairfax. About a dozen people, mostly older men and women, leaned close, their eyes glued to her.

She pressed a delicate hand to her collarbone and raised her eyebrows, her face full of animation, made only more exaggerated by the heavy stage makeup.

"And then he asked me if I could play piano!" She tittered, and the onlookers all chuckled, as though she'd just delivered the punchline to a hilarious joke. She beamed, clearly at ease as the center of attention.

We joined the back of the line for refreshments, and I glanced up at Prescott, who stood beside me, still holding my hand. I decided to make the best of the wait. "So... what was your favorite part of the play?" I smiled, running through all the best moments. I'd read the book over and over again, but it was a whole different experience to see it performed live. "I think the dancing was the best part. I'd love to go back in time and experience a Regency ball."

He grinned his adorable, lopsided smile, then scratched the back of his neck. "To be honest, I think I dozed off for half of it."

I chuckled. "No."

He winced. "Was it that obvious?"

"The snores gave you away a couple times."

His dark skin turned a deep plum color. "You must think I'm the worst date." He buried his face in his palm and groaned.

I nudged him with my shoulder, grinning. "Not at all. If it wasn't my favorite author's story, the dark would have knocked me out too." It wasn't entirely true, but I could tell he felt bad.

Prescott lifted his face. "I promise you it wasn't the play's fault, and certainly not the company." His dark eyes lingered on mine, before he let out a heavy breath. "I've been working long hours lately." His dark brows pinched together, and I raised my own.

"Not to pry, but... you have a new case?"

His expression grew clouded. "Something like that."

We shuffled forward as the line moved.

Well, that was cryptic. Then again, he was a detective inspector—he probably couldn't share all the details of his work with me. I took a deep breath and cast around for a new topic of discussion.

Of course my mind went blank, but we were saved from an awkward silence by a man who stood a few feet to my left. His booming voice made it impossible not to eavesdrop.

He wore a navy blue suit with a red rose tucked into the lapel. He was a shorter man, stocky, probably in his early sixties, with a gray goatee and slicked-back gray hair. Slick was the word for him... except for the clumps of tawny hair that clung to the back of his jacket. Someone owned cats. I grinned—I could relate. I had a cute black familiar of my own back home.

The man swirled the wineglass in his hand—an actual glass, not the plastic cups they were giving out at the bar. I raised my brow—did that mean he brought his own from home? Or did the bar keep a special glass just for him?

"My dear Mr. and Mrs. Winchester, how lovely to see you." His gravelly voice dripped with smarminess as he turned to the man who'd just strode up beside him, the actor who'd played the dashing Mr. Knightley. "Harvey, meet two of our most generous benefactors."

Harvey bowed his head and smiled politely, then leaned close to the man in the blue suit. "Richard, have you seen Petra?"

The actor, who already stood as tall as DI Prescott, rose on his toes to further gaze over the heads of the crowd in the lobby. "She's not out here."

"Yes, how very unlike her to miss out on basking in the adoration of her hordes of fans." The actress who'd played Jane Fairfax shot Harvey a snide look. "She must think she's too good to make an appearance." She sniffed. "If that's the case, then why should I bother sticking around, hm?"

Wow. Maybe the rivalry in the play between the two actresses extended to real life.

Harvey glared at her, and Richard reached out to stop her. "Elinor! Come now."

But she just huffed and threaded off through the crowd.

Richard shot the older Mr. and Mrs. Winchester a simpering smile. "The talent." He chortled, then reached for the older woman's cheek.

I frowned, startled. What was he doing?

He reached behind her ear, then withdrew a red rose, similar to the one in his suit. "Aha. A lovely rose for a lovely lady."

She grinned and took the flower, smiling at her husband.

Richard winked. "I used to be a magician in another life, you know, before I gave up the spotlight and took up my mantle as a director!"

I smirked and glanced back at Prescott, ready to smile with him at this man's absurdity. I frowned, though, as I found my date gazing off, his eyes unseeing and brows pinched together, as though lost in his own thoughts. I crossed my arms and pressed my lips tight together.

I'd really been looking forward to this date (well, with a healthy dose of anxiety mixed in) and had gotten all dressed up with Gus's help. I kicked at the red velvet carpet. I'd even worn heels! I was starting to think that Prescott must either have a really fascinating case... or maybe it *was* the company that was boring him.

Harvey turned back to Richard, his urgent tone again drawing my attention. "Elinor's right though. It's not like Petra to stay in her dressing room."

Richard raised a brow. "Did you check on her?"

Harvey shook his head as he continued to scan the crowd. "No, I just assumed that's where she'd be. I'm concerned she may be having a serious allergy attack. You saw her out there."

I bit my lip and glanced around the crowded lobby for the actress. So Petra *had* been suffering from allergies. This sounded like it might be serious.

The director, Richard, rolled his eyes, and turned back to the wealthy Mr. and Mrs. Winchester.

"As a director, one gets used to these dramatic actor types." He patted Harvey on the shoulder. "I'm sure she's all right, but why don't we go check on her?" He spread his arms wide. "Let's all go take a backstage tour, hm?" He raised his voice and waved an arm overhead. "Anyone who'd like to meet the star of the show, Miss Petra Cornflower? Follow me!"

With a flourish of his hand, he strutted back toward the theater. Yeah, and it was the *actors* who were the dramatic ones. Harvey huffed, then stalked off behind him, followed by the elderly Mr. and Mrs. Winchester and about a dozen other curious theatergoers.

From the other side of the lobby, cries sounded out, and the crowd parted for an odd-looking man, probably in his late thirties, who pushed people aside. His long trench coat billowed out behind him as he stomped straight toward me in his knee-high combat boots. I raised my brows. He certainly didn't look like a theatergoer...

I turned, half panicked, toward Prescott, to find that he'd paled.

Uh-oh. That wasn't a good sign.

2

CURTAINS

He sucked in a short breath, then glanced down at me. "Minnie, why don't you go ahead with the director. I'll catch up with you."

I smirked, then realized he wasn't kidding. Seriously? I glanced between him and the strange-looking guy stomping towards us. If he felt threatened, I was more inclined to stick close to him. My date didn't know it, but I was a witch—okay, a newbie witch, but I still had powers coursing through my veins. Powers that drew their source from the enchanted waters that Bath had been founded for. I could probably help him out if it came to a fight... maybe.

I opened my mouth to ask if he knew this guy, but Prescott cut me off.

"I'm sorry, but there's someone I need to have a word with."

I gaped. He wanted to have a word with that guy? I glanced once more at the strange man who now stood glowering at Prescott, just a few feet away, then nodded.

"Okay.... Sure." My heels sank in the thick, plush carpet

as I headed after the small group that had followed Richard into the theater. I stopped at the doors and glanced back.

Prescott and the strange man bent their heads close together, and my date wasn't happy. He scowled at the guy in the trench coat. "Why'd you come here?"

I probably shouldn't be eavesdropping, but my curiosity got the best of me. I backed up a few paces and ducked behind a group gathered around Bertram Kensington, the actor who'd played Mr. Elton.

I bit my lip and strained to hear their words over the cacophony of voices in the crowded lobby. I missed most of them, but one word very clearly met my ears.

"Vampires," the strange man in the trench coat hissed in a stage whisper.

My blood froze. Had I really just heard what I thought I had?

The group that stood in front of me broke apart, suddenly leaving a clear line of sight between me, my date, and his strange associate. They both turned to look at me and I jumped, then dashed to the theater doors and hurried down the center aisle to catch up with Richard, and as he'd put it, the tour group.

I joined the back of the group and followed them through a door beside the stage, barely aware of where I was walking.

Had that strange man really spoken about vampires to DI Prescott? Did this have something to do with the vampire hunter the vampire council had mentioned last month? Did this mean Fitz and Gus were in danger?

Richard led the way through the dark backstage, loudly pontificating about the history of the Theatre Royal and boasting about all the great plays he'd put on. I barely listened, too worried by the odd conversation I'd witnessed. I trudged along in a daze past ladders, racks of costumes, and bustling stagehands.

I nearly bumped into the couple in front of me when the group came to a stop.

Richard knocked on the door emblazoned with a plaque that read Petra Cornflower.

"Oh, Petra!" He simpered at the dozen or so of us in the group. "It's Richard."

"And Harvey!"

"And we've got some of your adoring fans here who are just dying to meet you!"

Silence followed.

Richard cleared his throat, his smile faltering. He knocked again. "Petra, darling?"

"See." Harvey huffed. "I knew it. I knew something was wrong."

A murmur of concern rippled through the group.

"Has something happened?"

"Did she leave already?"

The confusion snapped me out of my rumination. I hoped the talented actress was all right. A twinge of witchy intuition told me something was amiss. I hoped the poor gal hadn't gone anaphylactic from her allergies.

Richard fished a heavy key ring out of his pocket and flipped through several until he found the one he was looking for.

"Hurry," Harvey grunted.

Richard waved him off and then inserted the key into the door.

"Petra, dear! I hope you're decent." He pushed the door open, and I clambered with the rest of the theatergoers into the doorway.

Though quite small, the dressing room was at least private, unlike the shared one we'd passed that the rest of the cast presumably used. Petra was clearly a star. An enormous bouquet of probably six dozen red roses exploded from a vase on her vanity, lit by the bright globe lights that surrounded the mirror.

A rolling rack hung with costumes stood against the far wall, and to the right Petra lay on her side, eyes closed and apparently asleep on the worn leather sofa. She still wore the long Regency dress she'd worn during the play.

Richard snorted and perched on the cushion beside her.

He hammed it up by rolling his eyes. "Just like a star to nap on the job." He placed a hand on her shoulder and shook her gently. "Come now, Petra, it's time to say hello to your fans."

Harvey stood just inside the door, one arm folded across his chest, nibbling a thumb tip frantically. "Why isn't she responding?"

Richard spun on the cushion to face her and placed a hand on her back, shaking her more forcefully. Suddenly he yelped and recoiled, yanking his hands away from Petra's limp body.

He held his palms up so we all could see his left one drenched in red blood.

That certainly wasn't the result of allergies.

Harvey's eyes fluttered, then rolled back in his head, and he collapsed on the spot. Several women shrieked and screamed, and the entire crowd retreated from the dressing room, stampeding their way back toward me and shoving me back from the doorway.

Richard screamed, "Someone call the police! Petra's been killed!"

I stood frozen to the spot for a long moment, gasping for

air, then whirled and raced with the others back toward the lobby. I sprinted up the middle aisle of the theater. We didn't need to *call* the cops—I was on a date with one!

3

QUESTIONING

T he older, weathered DI O'Brien stomped into the theater flanked by uniformed officers. It'd been mere minutes since I'd rushed, panting, back to my date and informed him there'd been a murder.

O'Brien marched up to my date, pausing only long enough to scowl at me with those dark, intelligent eyes of his. He scrunched up his already deeply lined face.

"You again?"

I wiggled my fingers and managed a weak grin. "Yep, me again."

His gravelly voice grew more menacing. "Why do you always seem to show up at the scene of murders around here?"

He had a point. And I wasn't any happier about that than he was.

Prescott gave me a sympathetic look. "It's not Minnie's fault. We're actually here together on a date."

O'Brien raised his bushy brows.

"She was with the group who found the victim in her dressing room."

O'Brien returned his penetrating gaze to me, and I squirmed under it. I'd bet he got a lot of crooks to cave and confess just by glaring at them like that.

He grunted and addressed my date. "A word?"

They moved through the crowd of shell-shocked theatergoers to have a private word as uniformed officers broke everyone into small groups for interviewing. Others, toting evidence kits, pushed into the theater itself.

I hugged myself and rubbed my chilly upper arms. O'Brien was right. I'd been following death around, lately... or maybe death was following me? I shuddered.

As the police herded people into groups, the crowded lobby grew more open. I rose on my toes and looked around, but still didn't spot the dude in the trench coat who'd spoken with Prescott earlier. I frowned and sank back down on my heels. Who was that guy? And what was he doing talking to Prescott about vampires?

After about an hour and a half of waiting, giving my statement about what I'd witnessed, and then more waiting, DIs Prescott and O'Brien walked back into the lobby and called for our attention.

"If you've already given your statement, you're now free to go. Be sure to give your name to a uniformed officer at the door and make sure we've got current contact information for you in case we have more questions."

O'Brien planted his hands on his hips and glared around the lobby. "This is an ongoing murder investigation, and if you think of anything you've neglected to tell us, you're obligated to report it—immediately."

I curled my lip. Geez. He was treating us all like criminals.

Prescott, always more diplomatic, clasped his hands in front of him and flashed a charming smile at our anxious, tired group. "Thank you all so much for your cooperation. I know it's been a long, stressful night, but after you sleep on it you may remember something you'd forgotten. If so, please just get in contact with my partner or myself."

I smiled. They certainly had the good cop, bad cop routine down. Would it kill O'Brien to be a little friendlier?

As I'd already given my statement, I supposed I was cleared to go. I didn't want to leave before at least saying goodbye to Prescott, though. I threaded my way through the crowd, which was now filing out the exits, and rejoined Prescott and O'Brien. They stood in a circle with a few other people.

A uniformed officer held up a clear plastic capsule with a bit of red liquid lining the bottom in her gloved hand. "This one of yours?"

A young woman with curly brown hair and paint-stained overalls peered at the small packet. "I think so." She sniffled, her eyes red from crying. "Looks like one of the blood packets we keep on hand."

O'Brien choked. "Excuse me?"

The curly-haired gal held up a palm. "Calm down. It's theatrical blood. Corn syrup and red dye."

The officer turned to the detectives. "We found it in a wastebasket backstage."

I knew that stuff. My brother had used some one Halloween for his Dracula costume. It stained his face for days after—my mom couldn't get it off no matter how much she scrubbed. Kind of ironic now that my closest friends were vampires.

"And you are?" O'Brien glared at the gal in overalls.

She shot him a flat look, her eyes glassy. "Ariel. I'm the prop master."

O'Brien scowled at her. "And this is one of your props?"

She frowned. "I can't be sure, but probably." She shook her head, which sent her curls bouncing. "It doesn't make sense that you found it in a waste bin, though. We keep those on hand for other productions, but not *Emma*."

I snorted, which drew everyone's attention. My cheeks burned hot, and I flashed a sheepish smile. "Sorry. Just the idea of using blood packets for a Jane Austen play."

Ariel pointed at me. "Exactly."

The officer carefully placed the empty blood packet in a plastic evidence bag, then sealed it closed.

Prescott frowned. "If they weren't used for *Emma*, how did one find its way into the rubbish bin?"

"This is outrageous!"

We all turned toward the bar, where the actor who'd played the obnoxious Mr. Elton shouted at a waitress. "There's been a murder. I need a drink to calm my nerves."

The young woman looked uncomfortable. "I'm just packing up. The money bag's already been—"

"I don't care! I'm an actor! I work here! It should be on the house." The red-faced guy turned to the director, who dashed over. "Richard, tell her that actors don't have to pay for drinks."

The director gave him a stern look. "Now Bertram, we've discussed this, and this certainly isn't the time or place. You pay for your drinks, now."

The actor huffed, threw his hands in the air, and stomped off. Maybe there was something to Richard's lament earlier about the "talent" being needy.

Prescott waved the director over. "Mr. Leary? Could we speak with you, please?"

The director adjusted the rose in his lapel and strolled over, then bowed. "At your service, Detective Inspector."

I tried to catch Prescott's eye to share a knowing look—this guy was so dramatic. But my date was all business.

"We understand you unlocked Miss Cornflower's dressing room door. Who else had a key?"

Richard pulled his lips to the side. "Well, it's really a master key. It opens most of the doors in the theatre."

O'Brien grunted. "Hardly afforded the young lady privacy."

The prop gal shook her head, sniffling. "I can't believe she's gone."

Richard lifted a palm. "It was still a step above the common dressing room the rest of the actors used." He pointed at the gal in the overalls. "Let's see, Ariel has a key, the maintenance staff, the theater owners and manager, the head usher, the head of set dec, my assistant director, Petra herself, of course—"

O'Brien lifted a hand and cut him off. "Let me save you some time—was there anyone who didn't have a key to Miss Cornflower's dressing room?"

Richard shot him an apologetic look. "As I said, it was a master key. Anyone who had a need of getting into the theater, or opening it, had one. Our various teams often work odd hours, getting the stage ready or coming in for rehearsals." He winced. "And, though we've told them not to, I've heard that the keys are often loaned out. For instance, if the head of set dec needs to leave early, he might leave the key with one of his workers to lock up later."

O'Brien turned to Prescott and huffed. "That narrows our suspect list down to *everyone*."

Prescott nodded as he tapped away at his phone, taking notes. "If the killer didn't already have the key, it sounds like it could've easily been borrowed and copied."

O'Brien turned to the director. "Was Ms. Cornflower married?"

A muscle in the director's jaw jumped. He blinked. "No. She was single."

"Seeing anyone?"

Richard shrugged. "Not that I know of." He lifted a palm. "She was close with Harvey. He'd have a better idea."

Prescott looked up from taking notes. "Do you know her next of kin, so we can notify them?"

"I have her mother's number."

Everyone's gazes swung to Ariel as she pulled out her phone. She froze and sniffled. "What?"

Richard scoffed. "Why do you have Petra's mother's number?"

Her throat bobbed, and her cheeks grew red. "She, uh— she's an accountant. I had a tax question once." She showed the screen to Prescott, who jotted down the mother's information.

Curious as I was about the case—it sounded just as dramatic as the onstage action—I was also tired, and my feet hurt. Silly me, wearing heels.

I placed a hand gently on Prescott's arm when he'd finished. "I gave my statement earlier, so I think I'm going to head home, if that's all right with you? I'm sure you've got a lot more to do before you can call it a night."

He pressed his lips into a grim line, then looked from me to the door. "Let me just have a word with O'Brien. I'll walk you home."

"That's very gentlemanly of you, but it's all right." I waved him off. "It's only a five-minute walk back home to Gus's."

Prescott shook his head. "No, Minnie. You shouldn't be

out late at night. Not anymore, okay?" A muscle in his jaw twitched. "It's... It's just not safe."

I frowned. This sounded like more than just gallant concern for me. I supposed a woman had been killed in this very theater hours ago, but could it have to do with his conversation with that strange man in the trench coat?

What had Prescott so spooked?

4

THE SHORT WALK HOME

Prescott and I walked together through the dark streets of Bath back to my bestie Gus's gorgeous townhome. It wasn't quite the leisurely stroll by the river or romantic night on the town I'd been hoping for. Instead, Prescott seemed distracted and on edge. The heels of my stilettos clicked on the cobblestones as I had to nearly jog to keep up with him.

"Hey." I smiled when he looked around, startled, as though he'd almost forgotten I was with him. "Think we could slow down a little? Girl in heels here."

He flashed me a sheepish grin and slowed his pace. "Sorry about that. Just feeling anxious about this case, I guess." He fell into stride beside me and took my hand.

He wasn't the only one with anxious thoughts, though. I'd been trying to think of some way to get more information from him about that odd guy in the trench coat he'd been talking to. I couldn't help but be alarmed by the fact that the man had mentioned "vampires" to a detective when two of my closest friends were creatures of the night and I myself was a witch.

We strolled on at a more comfortable pace. The dark, cloudy sky hung low overhead, blotting out the stars and moon, and a heavy mist drifted along the narrow, winding streets.

I let out a dry chuckle. "Thanks again for walking me home." I gave an exaggerated shudder under my heavy wool coat. "It's actually a little creepy out tonight."

Prescott shot me a wan smile, then turned his vigilant gaze back straight ahead. He suddenly jerked to a stop in front of a dark alleyway, threw an arm across my chest, and with his free hand yanked his Taser from his belt.

I froze, listening hard, as my heart thundered against my rib cage. What had startled him? What threat had Prescott seen that I'd missed?

A gray cat darted out from behind a metal trash can and bounded across the street, meowing.

Prescott's shoulders sagged, and his arm dropped back to his side. Though my stomach was still a tight bundle of nerves, I managed a little chuckle. "My mom used to do that arm move in the car if she was braking too hard."

He groaned and shot me an apologetic smile. "I'm so sorry, Minnie." He grimaced. "Let's get you home?"

I nodded, took his hand, and we started off again at a quick pace. What had gotten into him? The detective was strung so tight, I thought he might break.

After another minute of striding through the dark streets in silence, Prescott shook his head. "How was she lying, when you found her?"

We took the next left, and after a puzzled moment, I figured out what he was talking about. "Petra?"

He nodded.

I sucked in a breath and thought back to that terrible

moment before Richard and I and the rest of the tour group had realized the actress was dead.

"She was lying on the couch, on her side."

"With her back to you?"

I shook my head. "No, with her face to us. She had her eyes closed, so we all assumed she was sleeping."

No wonder I'd had a witchy twinge of intuition that something was wrong.

"So you couldn't see the knife in her back?"

My stomach twisted. "That's how she was killed?"

Prescott blinked and looked down at me. "Sorry, I forgot I hadn't told you. We're not officially releasing that information yet, but yes. She was stabbed with a kitchen knife. We're pretty sure someone nicked it from the bar in the lobby. They used it for cutting up appetizers and hors d'oeuvres."

A car's headlights momentarily blinded me as it swung down the street towards us, then disappeared into the heavy fog.

I frowned. "No. We couldn't see the knife. She had her back to the back of the couch and the wall."

Prescott shook his head. "I just can't work it out. How and why would someone have stabbed her like that?"

I grimaced and edged closer to Prescott. Poor Petra. I was glad again to be escorted home on a night like this one.

"Stabbed in the front makes more sense." He huffed. "Toxicology will get back to us on the drugs in her bloodstream, but apparently the director, another actor, and the prop master all witnessed the victim taking antihistamines during the performance."

I nodded, my steps quick and short to keep up with my date. His pace seemed to speed up along with his thoughts. "Makes sense. She kept sneezing and sniffling, remember?"

Maybe he didn't—he'd slept through a lot of the performance.

Prescott nodded. "They all testified that the medicine made her extremely drowsy, so assuming our victim was already unconscious and in a heavy sleep, it's possible our killer snuck in without her waking."

He lifted his other palm. "But why would the killer roll her forward, stab her in the back, and then roll her back onto her side like that? Or, if she was conscious and our killer stabbed her in the back and she then collapsed, why lay her that way?"

I shrugged. "Maybe the killer wanted to buy some time? Make sure anyone who peeked in would assume she was just sleeping?" I was trying to keep up with Prescott, both physically and to follow his train of thought.

He nodded. "It's possible. But we didn't find any significant amount of blood anywhere else in the dressing room, except for on the couch, which suggests she was stabbed while lying there."

We turned down Union, and I spotted the steps up to Gus's townhome just down the row. "That is odd." It seemed our evening was going to end with talk about murder instead of romance, so I decided to just go with it.

"So it's most likely that someone stabbed Petra while she was already lying on the couch? Do you think she was so knocked out from the antihistamines that she didn't fight back?"

Prescott nodded. "That's my current theory."

I frowned as we slowed in front of Gus's townhome. "So someone wanted to make it appear as though she was still alive for as long as possible."

He nodded, his brow creased with deep thought.

"Hmm. It was probably someone in the crew or the audience then, right?"

He blinked at me. "What?"

I shrugged. "Well, the whole cast bowed and then almost immediately came out front to the lobby, right? The director too. They couldn't have done it right after the curtain fell, because it wouldn't have given Petra time to pass out." I lifted a palm. "They all have alibis." I frowned. "Though I do remember that one actress, Elinor, saying she wasn't going to stick around in the lobby if Petra wasn't."

Prescott gave me a small smile. "That's a good point. I'll check into Elinor's whereabouts, see if she stayed in the lobby the whole time or if she left. Thanks, Minnie."

I nodded and glanced behind me at Gus's front door. It was now or never. "Um... I actually wanted to ask you about that friend of yours—the one in the trench coat and boots?"

The streetlamps cast Prescott's features in shadow, but it seemed that his color drained. "He's not a friend."

I frowned. "Oh—I just thought, because you spoke with him, that—"

"It's work related." He shook his head. "Look, I'm sorry, I really can't talk about it."

My shoulders slumped with disappointment. Of course I should've known it wouldn't be easy to fish out information from a detective. On the other hand, he'd just blurted out a bunch of information about the actress's murder case, but he couldn't even tell me how he knew trench coat guy? My witchy intuition told me something odd was going on.

Prescott's eyes focused on my face, and he licked his lips. Again, I was struck by how exhausted he looked, his eyes bloodshot and skin gray. "I'm really sorry this has been such a... a weird date."

I gave him a tight grin. "I'm sorry, too."

He squeezed my hands, bent his head forward, and gave me a quick kiss on the cheek.

My face grew hot.

"I'm sorry, but I've, uh—" He took a step back and thumbed toward the theater. "I've got to get back."

I raised a hand. "I completely understand."

He shot me a grateful look. "Thank you. I'll, uh—I'll call you."

His tone didn't give me the most confidence. Then again, I wasn't sure I even wanted to go on another date with him, based on how this one had turned out. The whole murder thing wasn't his fault, of course, but I just wasn't sure there was much of a connection there.

With one last wave, he spun on his heel and sped back toward the theater, the mist swirling about his legs. I watched him go till he rounded the corner, then pulled my key from my clutch and opened the door with a heavy sigh.

Gus, my vampire bestie, looked up from where he lounged on the chaise in front of the fire across the room. "Date went that well, huh?"

I shot him a flat look as I toed my heels off, then let out a groan of relief as my feet spread out on the hardwood floor.

"You have no idea." I shrugged out of my wool coat, then hung it on the rack by the door. "Guess who found another dead body?"

5

VAMPIRES

I trudged over to Gus, who lounged on his favorite velvet chaise in front of the crackling fire. The hardwood creaked under my heavy steps, and I scooped my black cat familiar, Tilda, up before plopping down beside my vampire bestie. I let out a groan as I settled into the plush upholstery, the fire warming my back.

I curled my lip. "Who needs dates? It's so much more comfortable back here." I winced as I rolled my ankle. "And why did you make me wear heels? My feet are killing me."

I snuggled Tilda's fuzzy head under my chin and scratched her chest. She purred happily as Gus looked me over, lazily swirling his wineglass of blood. He lifted a blond brow. "Tell me what happened."

I sucked in a deep breath. "We went to dinner—Italian—then saw a play at the Theatre Royal."

Gus nodded his approval. "Bravo, Clive."

I frowned at him.

"What? That's his name, right?" Gus sipped his drink.

I bit my lip. "Yeah. It's just... the whole night I called him DI Prescott."

Gus choked and spluttered. "Why?"

I shrugged as Tilda stared at my vampire friend with flattened ears, alarmed by his coughing. "I don't know. That's how I think of him, I guess."

He shook his head, his brows pinched together in a look of pure pity. "That does not bode well."

I shook my head. "Nope. I mean, it was fine until this weird guy in a trench coat showed up after the play was over. He marched up to Pres— Clive." It sounded too weird, and I shook my head. "Prescott, and my date told me to follow the director for a backstage tour, that he'd catch up later."

Gus frowned. "He's losing points."

I raised my brows and leaned forward, Tilda still clutched to my chest. She meowed in protest. "That's not the worst part. I overheard the guy in the trench coat say something about vampires."

Gus stilled. "Did you, now?"

I nodded. "And then the director took us backstage to meet Petra, the lead actress, and we found her stabbed to death in her dressing room."

Gus's eyes widened.

I huffed. "And then trench coat guy was gone, and I tried to get more information out of Prescott about him, but he was being really cagey. And he could've just been being chivalrous, but he insisted on walking me home—he seemed afraid of me being out alone at night." I winced. "Gus, do you think he knows about you and Fitz and the others?"

Gus leaned back and crossed his ankle over the other knee. He sipped his blood, his blond brows pinched together in deep thought. "The council did say something about a vampire hunter sniffing about."

I nodded. "That's what I was thinking too. Could Prescott be working with a vampire hunter?"

Gus took a big swig of his drink. He was typically tight-lipped about vampire matters. I had no idea how old he was, though it was certainly hundreds of years older than the twenty-five he looked. He'd never told me how many vampires there were in Bath—or the world—and I knew very little about the vampire affairs he conducted late at night.

However, about a month ago I had helped him and my boss, Fitz, out by testifying on Fitz's behalf to the vampire council. A couple of unfortunate murders at Fitz's tearoom had unfairly cast him under suspicion, but I'd helped to clear his name. Now, it seemed, my vampire friends might have a new threat to face.

Gus licked his lips. "I'll have a word with Fitz about it." He gave me a solemn look. "I hate to ask, Minnie, but we may need you to stay close to Prescott and get as much information out of him as you can."

I grimaced, uncomfortable with the idea of faking an interest in Prescott just to get information from him. "Er... that might be difficult." I sighed through my nose. "He's super nice and handsome, but... I just don't think we're that compatible."

I lifted a palm, but Tilda nuzzled her head against my knuckle, reminding me to pet her. "Maybe it's just because I'm awkward—I mean, I haven't been in the dating game since Desmond and I got together."

Gus curled his lip at my ex's name, revealing a pointy fang.

"But it just felt—like it didn't flow. He wasn't that present with me, and I was all fidgety and... and I just want it to feel natural and fun and to light me up." My shoulders slumped. "I just don't think I see that with Prescott."

He raised a brow. "You mean unlike the way you can see it with a certain two-hundred-year-old vampire?" My neck and chest burned immediately hot, and my friend chuckled. "You're blushing!"

"No, I'm not!" I stared down at Tilda and her bright yellow eyes. I totally was.

"Minnie, you don't have to lead the young detective inspector on, but see if you can find a way to get information from him. I wouldn't ask if it weren't so important."

I quirked my lips to the side and glanced up at my friend's worried face. Gus almost never looked anything but cool, collected, and slightly amused. My stomach tightened with anxiety, and I nodded. "Of course I'll do it. I want to help keep you and Fitz safe." I shot him a small grin. "You're the best friend I've ever had."

Tilda batted at my hand, and I caught her tiny cat paw and rubbed the top of it with my thumb. "Along with you, of course." I nuzzled my nose against hers, and Gus rolled his eyes.

"Delighted I'm in such good company. Me and the fur ball you found in an alley."

I chuckled. "She's my familiar, and you know it."

He sniffed.

I meant it, though, about Gus being my best friend. When my ex broke it off and effectively fired me from the business we ran together at the same time, Gus welcomed me into his home. I'd had nowhere else to go.

And Gus had been there for me in college when I'd discovered my witchy powers and helped me navigate them. More recently, he'd connected me with Mim, the witch who ran a local potions shop and was giving me magic lessons.

Gus had even helped get me my job at Fitz's tearoom, which in turn had allowed me to stay here in the UK. I'd have been deported as soon as the divorce was finalized if it weren't for that. I owed Gus a lot, and though I wasn't sure how I'd do it, I wouldn't let him down. If Prescott was somehow involved with a vampire hunter, I'd get to the bottom of it.

6

THE TEA ROOM

The next morning, I sat on my usual stool across the butcher block island from Fitz, my vampire boss. I'd brought my laptop along, as well as Tilda —though she was understandably banned from the kitchen due to the cat hair. I tapped listlessly at the keys, ostensibly working on marketing for the tearoom.

Connecting with local tour guides and Jane Austen-themed clubs had stirred up a bunch of business for us. I'd also run ads to let customers know the space was available to reserve for bridal and baby showers. I had about four dozen emails and private messages to respond to, but I could barely focus on them. My mind was still whirring with last night's events.

With a heavy sigh, I snapped my laptop closed and plopped my face into my hands.

Fitz looked up from kneading bread dough and raised a brow. "Are you well?" He cleared his throat and dropped his eyes back to the dough. "Anything you'd like to discuss?"

I held back a grin. He knew I'd gone on a date with DI Prescott last night, and both of us had been dancing around the topic all morning. It was awkward... and also pretty cute. But that wasn't the subject I was obsessing over.

"Gus talked to you, right?" I looked around the kitchen, empty except for the two of us, and leaned forward, still lowering my voice to a whisper. "About the possible vampire hunter?"

Fitz pressed his lips together and lifted his dark eyes to mine. He shook a wavy strand of dark hair out of his eyes, and when that didn't work, dragged the back of his hand across his forehead. I bit back a smile at the streak of flour it left behind.

"He did." Fitz sighed through his nose and worked the dough with a bit more vigor. "We simply don't have enough information yet to say for sure, but it was smart of you to alert us about your suspicions." He caught my eye again. "Thank you, Minnie."

I gulped, my stomach a sudden flurry of happy nerves. Fitz slapped the dough on the floured table, then dragged the heel of his hand through it. He worked with his sleeves rolled up to his elbows, his hairy forearms dusted white. I couldn't have told you why that was so sexy... but it was.

I cleared my throat and shook myself. Focus, Minnie. I was half afraid he could hear my heart pick up its pace whenever he caught my eye or paid me a compliment.

"Of course." I bit my lip. "I want to help to keep you two safe." I dropped my gaze and picked at a bit of dough stuck to the table. "I'll see if I can find out more information."

Fitz grunted and pulled his lips to the side as he continued to knead. "I appreciate your concern, but if anything, *I* should be keeping *you* safe."

I sat up straighter and arched a brow. Here it came again: Fitz's old-fashioned sexism. He'd lived his prime years during the Regency, and while I appreciated his gentlemanliness, it often came at the cost of still thinking of us lady folk as the weaker sex. "Because you're the big strong man and I'm just the poor defenseless female?"

He paused his kneading long enough to shoot me a flat look. "*Because* I'm a vampire with superhuman strength."

"Oh." He had a point. I held up a finger. "Hey, I mean, I *am* a witch."

He gave me a little nod. "True. But you're still learning to use your powers. And if there is a vampire hunter about, they're going to be more dangerous than you can imagine."

I gulped. "Really?"

He looked up and held my gaze. "They lack our powers, but these hunters descend from long lines who have passed down their ancestral knowledge of our weaknesses. Because threats to our lives are so few and far between, we vampires tend to get complacent. It makes these hunters all the more dangerous." He frowned. "Well, few threats aside from those from other vampires, of course."

I huffed. He was, no doubt, referring to the vampire council, headed by his sire, Darius. He and Gus had explained that the council was basically a big pyramid scheme of vampires turning more vampires, all to serve Darius and his less-than-noble-hearted plans. The council was still looking for ways to get Fitz under their thumb and bring him back to the "nest," whatever that was.

I shuddered.

Fitz went on. "We tend to let our guards down, which makes these human hunters doubly dangerous." He shook his head. "I know Gus asked you to help, but that was an incredibly shortsighted, selfish blunder."

I raised my brows. That was about as harsh a rebuke as I'd ever heard out of Fitz's mouth.

"Let us take care of this, Minnie." He gave me a solemn

nod. "If we are dealing with a vampire hunter, I don't want you getting involved. It's too dangerous."

I bit my lip and stared into Fitz's dark eyes. Part of me wanted to protest—he and Gus were my friends. Maybe more, in Fitz's case, and if I could help, I wanted to. On the other hand, I'd barely begun lessons on using my powers and had only scratched the surface of learning about the magical world. I had no idea what tangling with a vampire hunter involved and felt in way over my head.

I jumped and spun on the stool as Calvin, a young, freckle-faced butler, pushed in from the dining room, dirty teacups and a crumb-covered tray in hand. He grinned his boyishly charming smile. "Hiya."

He flashed his eyes as the door swung shut behind him, once again muffling the clink of cutlery and murmur of voices from the tearoom. "It just picked up! We've got three orders for cranberry scones, four pots of tea, and a fresh loaf."

"On it, thank you." Fitz dusted his hands off on the kitchen towel hanging from his waist apron, then bustled off to the stove to put the kettles on.

Calvin set the dirty dishes in the deep farmhouse sink, then adjusted his coattails and ascot. All the butlers, including Fitz, dressed to the nines, right down to the white gloves.

He walked up beside me and shot me a sympathetic look. "Al told me what happened."

I froze for a moment, irrationally worried that he'd overhead Fitz and me talking about the vampire hunter.

He winced. "I'm so sorry you had to see that."

I relaxed. "Oh! Oh, the uh—the murder?"

Calvin pulled his lips to the side and nodded.

I shot him a grateful look. "Thanks. I wish I hadn't seen it. Can't get it out of my head, you know?"

"I do." Calvin gently squeezed my shoulder.

I frowned as I tried to shove away the image of Petra lying lifeless on her couch. "A real shame, too. She was wonderful in the play as Emma."

He shook his head. "Poor lady. I wonder who will replace her this evening."

I quirked a brow. "This evening?"

He nodded, a deep blush tinting his freckled cheeks pink. "I'm taking Rachel to see it tonight."

I was torn between delight and disbelief. He'd recently worked up the courage to ask out a girl in his class, and I was beyond pleased they were evidently still seeing each other. "That's wonderful. I'm so happy for you."

He looked down at his shiny brogues, blushing.

I shook my head. "But surely they're not continuing with the play? I mean... Petra was murdered just last night in her dressing room!"

Calvin shrugged. "They emailed to let us know there'd been a cast change due to an accident, but that the 'show would go on.'"

I huffed. That'd been no accident. Petra had been stabbed in the back! I'd heard that familiar saying before, but surely this was taking it a little too far.

Calvin gave me a sheepish grin. "How'd the date go?"

I frowned at him a moment, my mind so occupied with the vampire hunter and the murder of the lead actress that it took me a moment to process his words. "Oh, uh—" I darted a glance toward Fitz, who stood beside the stove, plating up a tray of scones and butter. Heat rose to my cheeks, uncomfortable with talking about my date in front of him.

"It was—odd. You know, with the whole murder thing." I crinkled my nose.

Calvin winced. "Yeah, of course. Well, hopefully your next date will be better." He gave me a hopeful smile.

Fitz's shoulders stiffened, and Calvin bustled back into the dining room to serve alongside the other butlers. I gulped—*awkward*.

Without turning around, Fitz spoke in a tone of forced lightness. "Apologies for eavesdropping, but... I'm sorry to hear the events at the theater put a damper on your date."

"Yeah..." I bit my lip. "To be honest, things weren't going exactly swimmingly even before that."

Fitz whirled around so fast it startled me. "Sorry to hear that."

I had to bite back a grin. He didn't sound remotely sorry. More like he'd just gotten some good news.

He had a little extra pep in his step as he carried a steaming kettle over to the workstation and poured the hot water into a teapot. He pursed his lips and shrugged. "Did something happen, or...?"

Thank goodness he kept his eyes down or he'd have caught me nearly laughing at him. Real casual, Fitz.

I cleared my throat. "No. I just don't think we're the most compatible." I sighed. "Don't get me wrong. We had a delicious dinner, and the play was wonderful. It was just good to go on a date." I scoffed. "It was my first in..." I shook off my attempt at mental calculations. "In a lot of years."

His lips tugged to the side. "However many it's been, I'm sure I have you beat."

His smile fell as he poured, and sympathy tugged at my heart. Fitz had told me he'd once been in love back in the Regency days, when he'd been a warm-blooded human. How many times in the hundreds of years since then had he experienced love again? Maybe our heartbreak was another thing we had in common.

Fitz jerked his head up and frowned, his expression darkening and his eyes intently fixed on the door to the dining room.

I froze. "What?" Surely the vampire hunter hadn't shown up here? His tense, still posture screamed danger to me. "Fitz, what is it?"

His eyes widened, and his gaze darted to me.

A moment later, Calvin burst into the kitchen, his brows pinched with concern. "There's a man here asking for you, Minnie."

I frowned. "Who?"

His throat bobbed. "Says his name is Desmond?"

Ice flooded my stomach. Desmond was here? How had my ex found me... and why?

7

WITCH HUNT

I shoved off the stool, hands shaking, and marched toward Calvin.

"Minnie, wait!"

I ignored Fitz and stomped through to the dining room.

The usual pleasant clinks and chatter of voices were drowned out by my own pounding heartbeat in my ears. My stomach felt sick with nerves, and I clenched my jaw so tight I was afraid I might break a tooth. The room swam when I spotted Desmond, pacing back and forth in the small entryway of the tearoom, tracking muddy footprints all over the previously shining hardwoods.

Meow! Tilda leapt out of her basket of blankets by the fire and sprinted under tables to my side. I shot her a grateful smile, and she stared straight up at me with her bright yellow eyes. I instantly felt stronger and more centered—my familiar always seemed to loan me more power.

I balled my trembling hands into fists and stalked up to Desmond. He jumped when he turned and found me right behind him, his blue eyes growing wider. His surprise instantly morphed into disdain, and he glared down at me, his lips pressed tightly together. He arched a single blond brow. "Minnie."

I darted a glance over my shoulder and found all five of the butlers—Calvin, Cho, Aldric, Leo, and Dominik—staring. My cheeks grew hot, and I turned back to Desmond. "Let's step outside."

He sniffed. "Why? So I don't embarrass you at your place of work?" He sneered as he looked around. "So you're a waitress now?"

No. I was a marketing manager, but it wasn't any of his business and who cared if I was a waitress? A rush of hot anger flooded my chest and throat. When I'd met Desmond, I'd found him charming, almost princely. How had I missed how arrogant and selfish he was?

I frowned. It was probably the British accent—it always made people seem more refined.

I flashed my eyes at him. "What are you doing here?"

"You ignored my text, so I tracked you down."

I made a disgusted noise in the back of my throat. "You're stalking me now?"

He rolled his eyes. "Oh, grow up. You're posting this place all over your social media. Not like it was hard to find you."

I huffed. "Grow up?" That was rich from the man who'd run off with his hairdresser and was now bullying me at my place of work. "What do you want, Desmond?" I ground out between gritted teeth.

"You know what I want."

I scoffed. "I really don't."

He leaned forward and bared his teeth. "Break the curse you put on me, or I'll make your life miserable."

Tilda hissed, and he jumped back. He curled his lip at my familiar. "On your way to being a crazy cat lady, I see."

My hands trembled at my sides. "I'm going to say this once." My chest heaved. "I didn't hex you. You need to leave."

He folded his arms and stepped his feet into a wider stance, as if planting them, and sneered. "I'm not going anywhere. We can play that game if you want to."

He lifted his chin and glanced over my head, behind me, raising his voice so that it carried to the packed dining room. "You're a witch and you hexed me, and I demand you undo it right now!"

A crash sounded behind me, and I spun as Dominik slammed a loaded tray onto the nearest table and stalked toward us, loosening the ascot at his throat. Dom was enormous, with shoulders so broad I was often surprised he could fit through doorways. I shot him a grateful look as he stood beside me and glowered at my ex.

"What did you call her?"

Desmond paled, and his throat bobbed. He staggered back a couple of steps toward the door.

Dominik sniffed and curled his thick lips. "That's what I thought. Get out."

Desmond edged back until he stood with one hand on the doorknob. "Don't threaten me. I'll call the police."

Cho stomped up behind me. He placed his hands on my shoulders and squeezed. "Is this jerk your ex?"

I nodded, my throat too tight to speak.

Leo came up on my other side and cracked his knuckles. He was stocky and buff and had plenty of attitude. "Oh, look. A human punching bag."

Calvin rushed up with Aldric a moment later. Calvin held his cell phone up. "I'll call the police if you don't leave."

Aldric, whose calm, deep voice and unflappable demeanor always made me feel relaxed, now shot Desmond a menacing grin. "Sir. You've made things unpleasant." Somehow Al's politeness came off even more threatening than Leo and Dominik's direct challenges.

Desmond gulped, then turned to me and glared. "You know, I knew you'd be bitter, but have a little dignity, Minnie."

Dominik lunged forward, but Cho and Aldric caught his arms and held him back. I shook my head at him. Dominik had grown up in a rough household and turned to petty crime as a young kid to scrape by. Fitz had hired him on and gotten him a special visa to stay in the country, but he needed to keep his nose clean and out of trouble with the law. Otherwise, he risked being deported back to Romania.

I shot the ridiculously handsome Dom a wan smile. "Thank you. But trust me—he's not worth it."

I whirled to face Desmond. "What's this all about anyway? What 'hex' do you think I put on you?"

He scowled. "I know you made her break up with me."

"Ha!" I couldn't help the cheerless laugh that burst out of me. Unbelievable. First he left me for another woman, then had the gall to accuse me of causing their breakup?

I shook my head. "You did that all on your own." The petty part of me couldn't help but be a little amused by the situation. I mean, I wasn't about to call on supernatural forces to make misfortune befall my ex, but I could at least revel in it a little when he got his comeuppance.

Desmond pointed a trembling finger at me. "This isn't over, Minnie. You're going to make this right, or so help me, I'll—"

The color drained from his face, and his mouth fell open in a round O of horror.

I turned, and my eyes widened. The lamplights flick-ered, and the cheerful flames in the fireplace went out. I crouched down and scooped Tilda into my arms, hugging her close to my chest.

The diners froze, teacups half raised to their lips, as did the butlers, completely motionless. The swinging door to the kitchen banged open, and Fitz floated out, his toes dangling above the floor. It was as if the world drained of color, going black and white, Fitz's skin pale, his dark eyes blazing.

As he drifted closer, the sense of dread and heaviness thickened. At least, I imagined it did for Desmond, who cowered, whimpering. I was simply in awe. I had no idea how powerful Fitz was before this. Could all vampires do that? Could Gus? As he floated past me, his fangs bared and shadow somehow looming ten feet tall, Fitz darted a quick glance at me and winked. I had to stifle a smirk.

He loomed over Desmond, and when he spoke his voice came out deeper, more resonant, echoing all around us. "You will leave this place and never return, and you will leave Minnie alone!"

Desmond froze, his eyes vacant and jaw slack. He gave a slow nod.

Fitz pointed at the door, which flew open. "Now go."

Without another glance at me, my ex stumbled out and away, down the street.

I opened my mouth to ask Fitz what had just happened, but he cut me off. "I glamoured them. No one will remember it." His feet settled back firmly on the floor, and he adjusted his ascot.

Gus had let me in on the secret of glamouring. Vampires could magically hypnotize people to do and feel what they wished. I'd only seen it in action a few times, and I'd had no idea it could be powerful enough to mesmerize an entire room of people.

"Will Desmond—?"

Fitz, suddenly looking quite drained, ran a hand over his damp forehead. "I can't guarantee he won't harass you again, once the glamour wears off." He gave me a weak grin. "But there's a chance I scared him enough to keep him away."

He cleared his throat. "Apologies for not coming to your aid sooner. I've been attempting to learn from you and allow you the agency to take care of yourself." He bowed his head. "I hope you understand the intent of my intervention was merely to support you and keep that bloody shabbarroon from bothering you."

Still shaken, I couldn't hold back a grin. "That *what*?"

Fitz's face softened as he grinned back. "When I get angry, I'm afraid I regress to Regency slang."

I chuckled, and he did, too.

Slowly the color returned to the room. The birds chirped outside again, and the crackling fire roared to life. As if they'd simply been put on pause, the diners returned to eating, sipping tea, and chatting, and the butlers shook themselves.

Dominik huffed, and Cho and Aldric released him. He stomped out the front door and looked down the street after Desmond, then marched back inside. "Good riddance."

Calvin held up his phone. "Should I still let the police know?"

Fitz shot me a questioning look, but I shook my head. "No, thanks though." I grinned at the butlers. "Thanks all of you for having my back." I gave Fitz a significant look, and he acknowledged it with a nod.

My boss's throat bobbed, and even for a vampire he looked pale. "I must be getting back to it."

The butlers jumped and whirled. Cho looked Fitz up and down. "When did you get here?"

Fitz ignored him and dragged his feet back to the kitchen.

I bit my lip. All that glamouring and floating must've really taken it out of him.

Cho threw an arm around my shoulders and hugged me tight to his side. "Nobody comes in here insulting our Minnie."

My cheeks grew warm. These guys had really stood up for me—that meant a lot. When Desmond and I split up, I basically lost all my friends. They'd been his originally anyway, since we'd moved back to his nearby hometown. Even though I'd wanted to stay here in the UK, I'd been afraid it might be lonely, since all my family was back in the States. I glanced around at the butlers—guess I didn't need to worry, though.

We all returned to the dining room together. Leo walked behind me, punching one hand into the other. "I'd have liked to pummel his face. I can't believe he called you a witch!"

My stomach tightened. We'd grown close, but there was still a lot these guys didn't know about me. Would they still be my friends if they knew the truth about my powers?

"Yeah." I let out a dry chuckle. "Crazy."

8

MIM

fter the initial shock of being confronted by Desmond—at my place of work, no less—wore off, anger replaced it. Over the next several hours, my ruminations grew darker and angrier. How dare he? And did he seriously think I was the reason his new relationship had ended? It couldn't be his pig-headed, selfish ways—no! It must be witchcraft!

When I grew too restless and realized work just wasn't going to happen, I thanked Fitz and the butlers for standing up for me again, then packed up my laptop, scooped up Tilda, and left. I marched through the long shadows of the late afternoon over to Mim's potion shop.

To any human passerby, the storefront appeared to be just another stretch of honey-colored stone wall. But to magic folk like me, dried bunches of herbs and flowers crowded the shop window, along with beeswax candles, a handmade broom, and a jumble of glass jars in all sizes and colors.

The bell above the door jingled as I threw it open and

stomped inside. Mim glanced over her shoulder at me, and her pale blue eyes widened in surprise.

"Minnie! Tilda!" Her face broke out into a broad smile, wrinkling at the corners of her sparkling eyes. "Good to see you, pet."

Her faint brows drew together as she backed down the wooden step stool she'd been perched on, stuffing small cubbies full of various herbs and plants. "Did we have a lesson today?"

I huffed. "No! But I need one. I want you to teach me a spell or a potion that'll get someone to leave you alone—forever!" I stormed over to the raised wooden counter littered with mortars and pestles, bunches of dandelion flowers, and a cork-stoppered cobalt-blue bottle. I dropped my big leather bag next to the stool I usually sat on during our monthly lessons, then placed Tilda atop it, and paced up and down the small, crowded shop.

Normally, the lovely smells of lavender, sage, and rosemary that permeated the place calmed me down. The low, cottage-beamed ceiling, the crackling fire, and Mim's motherly presence were usually a balm that soothed any worries. And it certainly made focusing on my magic easier. But today, my nerves were shot.

Mim watched me for a moment, her brows raised and lips pulled to the side in an infuriating smirk. "Anyone in particular?"

"My ex, Desmond." I halted my pacing long enough to face her and throw my hands up. "He showed up at the tearoom, called me a witch in front of everyone, and demanded I break the 'hex' I put on him."

Mim's expression darkened. "Tosser."

"Exactly!" I let out a frustrated shriek, then returned to my pacing. "Can you believe him? The nerve!"

Tilda, perched atop the wooden stool, watched me intently with those big yellow eyes and let out an angry yowl.

I gave her a grim nod. "Thanks, Tilda." My black cat familiar always knew when to lend me a little extra strength —it was comforting to know she always had my back. Maybe I should've had her bite Desmond's ankles.

Mim pressed her lips tight together, threw her long sky-blue scarf over her shoulder, then bustled behind the counter. "Hold on, dear, I've got just the thing." She rose on tiptoe to reach the wooden cabinet above the small sink, her long skirt swaying above the stone floor, then returned to me with a small, dusty brown bottle. She unstoppered it, poured me a generous glass of the amber liquid, then pushed it across the wooden counter to me. "Drink up. You'll feel better."

I pulled the cool glass closer and raised a brow. "Is this some kind of potion?"

Mim smirked. "It's whiskey, so pretty much." She winked.

I sighed, took a sip, and winced as the liquid burned my throat. "Ack!" I ran my tongue over the roof of my mouth.

"Psh." Mim reached over and grabbed the glass, sipped from it, then pushed it back to me. "This is the good stuff."

Tilda stood and placed one delicate paw on the counter, leaning forward to gingerly sniff at the glass. She instantly recoiled.

I spoke out of the corner of my mouth to her. "I'm with you."

"Now." Mim rested her elbows on the counter and laced her fingers together, studying my face. "About this spell to make your ex leave you alone. You're sure that's what you want?"

I huffed. "Yes! Fitz scared him off earlier, but I want to make sure he never comes back."

I smirked as I remembered the flickering lights and hovering act Fitz had put on. At least, I thought it was mostly an act. Something told me Fitz had been in control of himself, but if he hadn't... A shiver ran down my spine. For as genteel and mannered as Fitz was, it was both terrifying and attractive whenever I caught glimpses of the feral vampire underneath.

Mim raised a brow. "Scared off?"

I gulped and considered what to tell her. Vampires kept their existence under wraps to such a degree that most of the magical world believed there was only a single vampire left. I didn't know if Mim knew about vampires or that Gus and my boss were ones, so I decided to skirt around the truth. "Yeah. My boss and coworkers stood up for me. Told him never to come around again."

Mim gave an approving nod. "Good chaps."

I smiled. "They are." I sobered as I remembered the ridiculous charges Desmond had leveled against me. "My ex accused me of breaking up his new relationship—as if he wasn't more than capable of doing that on his own." I shook my head. "I'm ready to move on and leave him in my past."

Mim gave a slow nod, her brows raised in that annoyingly mysterious way most witches had about them. It told me she knew something I didn't but would be leaving it up to me to figure out.

I huffed. "I am. In fact, I went on a date the other night." I frowned. "Of course, it didn't go amazingly... ended in an actress being killed and my date having to go on duty."

Mim sucked in a breath. "That young woman who'd starred in *Emma*, you mean, over at the Theatre Royal?" She clicked her tongue. "Poor thing. I read about it in the paper."

She winced. "And rather unlucky for you, too. Hm, well." She rose and came around the counter to give my shoulder a gentle squeeze. "I'm proud of you for getting back out there again."

She pressed her lips together and gave me a sympathetic look. "But I'm sorry to say that no spell is going to repel your ex when you still have so much anger and hurt connecting you two."

My mouth fell open. "What? So this is my fault he's coming around?"

She frowned. "Oh dear, no. That's all on that wanker ex of yours." She huffed. "I have half a mind to turn him into a frog."

I brightened. "Could you?"

She let out a heavy sigh. "Sadly, no. Well, not without some unexpected and terrible consequences. Usually how those spells go." She came around to my other side and scooped Tilda into her arms.

"You see, that's why we work so hard to clear your mind and focus on your magic. If other feelings are mixed in, it can lead spells to mutate or backfire in unpredictable ways. I'm afraid if you tried a repelling spell right now, all that— quite understandable and justifiable—anger you feel might just as likely attract him to you as send him away."

"Grr." My shoulders slumped as that rush of anger and adrenaline dried up, and only a watery sense of exhaustion remained. "Not what I want to hear, but I get it."

"Come now, my darling. Grab your things and come along." She spun to check the cuckoo clock on the wall. "Don't want to be late."

I bent over and grabbed my enormous leather tote. "Late? For what?"

Mim shifted Tilda in her arms to grab her long wool

coat, which hung on an iron hook by the door. "For the spring equinox celebration, of course." She leveled me a stern look. "And it's about time you attended a coven gathering."

She grinned. "Also, there's a lot of drinking, so you're going to be my designated driver home."

Great.

9

THE EQUINOX

It only took Mim about half an hour to drive me, her, and Tilda through the deepening dusk over to the nearby village of Stanton Drew. Mim's little well-loved blue Vauxhall Astra flew along the highway roads, past rolling hills of green farmland dotted with white sheep and sectioned into a patchwork of fields by hedgerows. She'd turned on the headlights, and the sky had deepened to an inky blue when she pulled down a dirt road. We bumped along next to a vast field and mooing cows kept in by a low stone wall.

"Why are we going to Stanton Drew for the celebration?" I scratched under Tilda's chin, and she purred, the tip of her tail swishing.

Mim leaned forward and peered into the dark lane. A row of low stone buildings with tiled roofs appeared on the left. "Ah. Nearly there. Because of the stones, dear."

I raised a brow. "What stones?"

She tsked. "The standing stones. You really need to learn more about your witchy heritage." She reached over and patted my leg. "This'll be a good learning opportunity for you."

I snorted. "That, and you needed a designated driver, apparently."

She smirked. "That too."

She slowed the car down in front of a stone pub, the only building in the row with lights on. About ten women gathered around a wooden picnic table out front, and the door stood open, golden light and music spilling out. A sign above the door read Druids Arms Pub.

Mim guided the car through a narrow gap in the fencing and cruised slowly over the grassy field. She pulled up alongside about two dozen other vehicles in the makeshift parking lot, their noses all pointed at the low stone wall which bordered the lane. A row of buildings, with the pub in the center, lined the other side of the road.

Mim killed the engine and unbuckled her seat belt. "We're here."

I curled my lip. "*Where?*"

I leaned forward to peer at the pub. It sat in the middle of some cow fields, which were in turn in the middle of nowhere. Mim just chuckled, and I followed her out of the car and across the field without any enthusiasm.

I was supposed to be back in Bath, helping Fitz and Gus figure out if that guy in the trench coat was the rumored vampire hunter. Tilda squirmed, so once we jogged across the narrow lane and approached the women outside the pub, I set her down.

When I'd first learned I was a witch in college, I'd confessed my powers to Gus, who at that time I thought was just my fun new bestie. He'd confessed he was a vampire and had introduced me to various witch covens he knew.

None of them had been quite the right fit, and it honestly made me feel like even more of an outcast. I was already an American and a witchy late bloomer—I wasn't really looking forward to going through that experience yet again with new witches.

Mim leaned close and spoke out of the corner of her mouth. "Stop fidgeting."

"I'm not." I huffed and stopped nibbling the sleeve of my sweater, dropping my arm to my side again.

"Now these women are all members of various local covens. The spring equinox celebration, or Ostara as some call it, is a time when we all gather at places of particular power."

I shot her a disbelieving look. "Like the Druids Arms Pub? I thought you said we were going to some standing stones."

She ignored me. "Mingle. Take this opportunity to see if you resonate with any of the covens."

Based on past experience, I wasn't going to hold my breath. But I'd try to keep an open mind.

We stopped in front of the picnic table, Tilda weaving through my ankles, as a middle-aged woman with an enormous barn owl perched on her shoulder and a pint in her hand leaned forward. The whole table leaned with her, hanging on her every word.

"So then I says to him, 'A broom's not the only thing I ride well!'" She slapped the table as all the witches broke into raucous laughter. The older lady on the bench closest to me hiccupped, and I eyed the mounting pile of empty pint and shot glasses on the table. Looked like Mim wasn't kidding about needing a designated driver. These witches liked to party.

As the bawdy laughter quieted down, Mim cleared her throat, and the lady with the owl on her shoulder looked up. "Ah, Mim!" She raised her half-empty glass, and Mim nodded back.

"Morgan. Good to see you. Happy Ostara."

"Happy Ostara!"

The older lady's gaze drifted to me, and she narrowed her eyes. "And who's this? Don't recognize you, lass."

Mim nudged me, and I cleared my throat. Should I curtsy? I didn't know the proper witch customs. "I'm Minnie Wells."

The owl blinked its big dark eyes at me, and I gulped, oddly intimidated by it. Tilda nuzzled my leg, and I felt instantly more calm, the tightness in my chest relaxing.

"Minnie short for something?" The owl and its witch blinked in tandem.

"Uh, yeah. Minerva."

The witch snorted and turned to the gal who sat across the table from her. "Water witch, I bet."

I frowned. "Er... yeah. How'd you know th—"

Mim wrapped an arm around my shoulders and tugged me toward the open door to the pub. "I'll be back once we make the rounds."

The owl witch saluted with her pint glass, and the table fell back into lively conversation.

Mim nodded her greetings at the beefy bald guy who sat on a stool in front of the door, and he nodded back. She guided me into the warm, noisy pub, which was packed with women.

Lively instrumental Irish music blared from the jukebox, and to our left, the rustic wooden tables were crowded with women of all ages and a few men, many more standing around in small groups chatting and laughing. Various owls, cats, ravens, and even a few foxes joined the crowd, perched on overhead beams or sitting beside women on benches. I assumed that these, like Tilda, were witches' familiars. I smiled—how cute.

Mim led the way to the small bar, and I hung back as she squeezed between two ladies on wooden stools. As she flagged down the bartender, I glanced around. The place looked ancient with its low, wooden-beamed ceiling, the slightly crooked walls covered in chipping white plaster. I frowned as I spotted a framed, weathered proclamation from 1623 "Casting out all witches and deviles from the hamlet."

"Minnie—you want anything?"

I startled and turned back to face Mim. The bartender, an older guy with a big mustache, raised his bushy brows at me.

She followed my gaze to the sign and chuckled. "Ah. Inside joke." She grinned. "I got the fish and chips—highly recommend them."

I nodded, suddenly remembering it'd been a while since I had lunch and my stomach was empty. "Sounds good. Make it two, please."

Mim finished our order and walked away from the bar with an ice-cold pint in hand. I could've done with a drink—except I was driving apparently. She tipped her head toward an open door at the back, then leaned close and shouted to be heard. "Let's head out back!"

Mim stopped to greet a few women on the way out, and when we finally stepped into the dark, cool night, it was like a breath of fresh air after the warm, muggy pub.

"Well, here it is. The Cove and the site of our spring equinox celebration."

"The Cove?"

She led me and Tilda past women gathered on fallen logs they were using as benches, little bonfires, a picnic table of women decorating what looked like Easter eggs, another group dancing and laughing barefoot in a circle, and finally to a small semicircle of standing stones. Mounds of decorated eggs lay piled at their bases.

It was a beautiful, mysterious scene, with the pub's back garden only separated from the surrounding fields by a low wooden fence. We could see for miles, and besides the pub and the bonfires, the only lights came from a twinkling village far off in the distance and the bright stars overhead. Closer, an old stone church with a tall square tower and surrounding cemetery loomed in the night.

Mim swept an arm toward the big, moss-covered stones, which stood a few feet taller than me and must've weighed tons. "These three circles form the Cove." She pointed to our left. "Out that way, there are a couple more groupings. The big one is actually one of the largest stone circles in the country—kind of a local secret. We like to keep it that way. Let everyone get their kicks at Stonehenge, you know?"

I nodded. "Sure."

Tilda cautiously stalked forward and sniffed at a pile of nearby eggs.

"Our ancestors used to celebrate all the major occasions of the natural world at those sites, and here as well."

I lifted a brow. "Why don't we gather at the bigger sites?"

She winked a sparkly eye. "It's cold, and they have great food and beer here. Plus, the cows don't get in the way."

I bit back a chuckle. "Sounds reasonable."

Mim took a sip of her beer, then nodded at the stones. "Local folklore says that the Cove represents a parson, bride, and bridegroom who were all turned to stone because their wedding party danced past midnight into Sunday and the Devil turned them to stone."

I frowned. "And that's... bad? The dancing part?"

Mim smirked. "It's a rumor that *may* have been started by witches. We let them think it's bad. Keeps them from interfering in our late-night rituals."

I grinned. "Tricky."

She chuckled.

I couldn't deny though, there did seem to be some ancient power bound in these enormous, bizarre stones. "So... how do I celebrate spring?"

Mim finished a sip of beer and nodded. "It's all about new beginnings. It's a good time to work fertility magic or spells that take some time to come to fruition. Hence the eggs—we decorate them, a symbol of fertility, and offer them to the stones. It's a good time for fire magic as well, and dancing and celebrating being alive."

She squeezed my shoulder. "I'm going to say hello to some old friends. Why don't you wander about?"

I bit my lip, anxious at the thought of her leaving my side. I didn't know anyone or what I was doing. "But I don't—"

She gave me a warm smile. "You don't have to participate if you don't feel comfortable. Just observe at least. Get a feel for things." She winked at my cat. "You keep an eye on her for me."

Tilda meowed, as if in response.

I frowned. I still hadn't quite worked out if Mim could actually speak to my cat...or if that was even a thing.

I nodded and waved as she wandered off into the dark and left me standing in front of the stones, alone with my cat. I sighed and looked down at Tilda. "Sorry you're not matched up with a better witch."

She looked up, flattened her ears, and meowed as if to tell me not to talk about myself that way. I smirked. "I suppose you're right. No point in getting down about myself. I'm still learning. Come on, Tilda...let's mingle."

My familiar trotted along beside my ankles as I wandered through the chilly back garden. I spotted an empty spot at a picnic table where a few witches who looked about my age decorated eggs.

I shrugged, then gestured at the empty bench spot. "May I?"

A gal with long black hair and cute vintage glasses glanced up. "Of course." She scooted over to make even more room for me.

I grinned and sat, my stomach a bundle of nerves. "Thanks."

Tilda sprung up onto the bench beside me and lifted her nose to peek at the piles of eggs on the table.

The gal with short blond curls who sat across from me smiled. "Want to decorate an egg?"

"Oh, sure." I hadn't done that since I was a kid at Easter.

She pushed the bowl of hard boiled eggs at me then pointed out the various bowls of colored water, lit by candlelight. "We only use natural dyes from beets and that sort of thing, of course."

The gal with the black hair and glasses pointed at a jar of glitter. "And if you're feeling glamorous..."

I chuckled, then sucked in a breath as I admired her work. She'd dyed her egg black, then decorated it with glue and vibrant green glitter in pretty swirls.

"I'll be happy if mine turns out half that pretty."

She grinned and the blond across from me shook her head. "Nobody's turn out as good as Louisa's, she's a makeup artist."

"Oh, cool."

We fell into chatting as I dyed my egg a deep purplish red, then glued on gold rhinestones. I learned that the young women lived in nearby towns and that the makeup artist, Louisa, came from a long line of witches. The blond, Anita, had only discovered her powers when she was in her early twenties, like me. It made me feel better to know that not every witch had been practicing magic since they could walk. Once I'd finished my egg, Louisa pointed back at the cluster of stones that made up the Cove.

"Now, you just place your egg at the base of one of the stones as an offering."

Anita grinned, her eyes crinkling at the corners. "You can offer up a little prayer if you like, asking for a certain something to happen and bloom with Spring."

I rose and plucked up my egg. "Thanks for the help." I raised my brows. "Here goes nothing!"

They wished me good luck, and as Tilda and I threaded our way back to the stones, I felt lighter, more at home. I'd made some witch friends! And they were nice and not at all scary. Plus, Anita was pretty new to magic, like me. Maybe I wasn't as behind as I thought I was.

I stood in the dark before the looming stones and held my decorated egg in my hands. What to ask for? I bit my lip. I could ask for help discovering the identity of the man in the trench coat, or for Petra's killer to be caught. But my gut told me it should be something more personal.

I blew out a breath. I knew what I'd ask for.

I stepped forward, crouched in front of the center stone, and placed my egg at its base among the pile of others.

"Um...not sure if I'm doing this right..." I murmured. "But, I want to become a better witch. I want my powers and confidence to grow. I want to bloom into my abilities." I pictured daffodils and tulips pushing up through rich, dark soil and their bright flowers unfolding in the sun.

I rose and backed away. Was something else supposed to happen?

Tilda blinked up at me with her bright yellow eyes, stalked forward and sniffed my egg.

I lurched forward. "Don't eat it!"

She shot me a flat look, then licked the egg, and strutted away, tail in the air. I frowned. Was that Tilda's version of an offering?

I looked up from my cat and found a slight woman with curly, shoulder-length hair approaching out of the darkness, a single decorated egg in her hands. Her shoulders drooped and she hung her head, so I couldn't see her features in the dark, but she looked familiar....

She dragged her feet over to the stones and knelt in front of them, murmuring a few words, and then rose and spun to face me. In the dim light filtering out the pub door, wet streaks tracked down her cheeks—tears. She sucked in a breath as our eyes met, then ducked her head and turned to leave.

Suddenly, I placed her. "Hey—you're the prop master at the theater, right?"

She stopped, and her eyes narrowed as she searched my face. "Do I know you?" She sniffled and dragged the back of her hoodie sleeve under her nose.

I walked closer, and Tilda meowed and trotted over to my side. "Not really. I was at the play the other night when..."

Her throat bobbed, and she dropped her glassy eyes to the ground. "Oh."

I frowned and pressed my lips together, concerned. Was that why this young woman was so upset and crying?

Because of Petra's death? She'd had Petra's mother's number in her phone. "Were you and Petra close?"

She sucked in a breath. "Not recently."

Interesting answer. Did that mean they'd once been close and had a falling out? Was this grief... or perhaps guilt over killing the actress?

I cast around for a way to get more information out of her. "I'm Minnie, Minnie Wells. I'm new to the area. So... you're a witch too?"

She huffed and looked up, shooting me a flat look. "No. I'm just here for the fish and chips."

I raised my brows, and she seemed to deflate.

"Sorry." She scrubbed a hand over her face, then raked her fingers through her wild curls and looked around. "I'm just having a really hard time with Petra's death." She pressed her lips together and gave me a contrite look. "I'm Ariel Morgenstern." She blinked and recognition lit up her dark eyes. "Hey—I remember you now. You're close with that detective, right?"

I gulped, and my cheeks flushed hot. How to answer that? We'd been on a date, but I wasn't sure there'd be another. "Um... kinda. Why?"

She stepped closer and jabbed a finger at me, her eyes wide and blazing. "Tell him to look into Richard."

I blinked in surprise. "The director?" The dude with the cheesy magician tricks?

She nodded and bared her teeth. "He was always weirdly possessive of Petra. Trust me—he should be the top suspect." She sniffled, her face suddenly crumpling. "I have to go," she choked out before burying her face in her hands and dashing off into the night.

I dipped down and scooped Tilda into my arms, then stood watching after Ariel until she disappeared into the deep shadows of the back garden. I'd make sure to pass the message along to DI Prescott—at least that would give me a good excuse to see him again and try to fish out more information about that odd man in the trench coat he'd been speaking with.

10

THE STATION

The next morning, around midday, I walked the winding cobblestone streets of Bath over to the police station. Though I still bundled up in my thick wool coat and wool tights, the sun glinted off the stately honey-colored townhomes, birds chirped in the trees, and green shoots poked up from the soil, promising beautiful flowers to come. I grinned to myself. Maybe all those decorated eggs and witches raising their pints to Ostara last night had ushered spring right in.

Good thing it was so cheery out. I shuddered as I passed the spot on the street where I'd been abducted a couple of months ago on my way to give DI Prescott and his partner some information about a case. It'd been dark and stormy that night—now a woman with a young child in tow smiled at me as they strolled past. Much less scary this time around.

I spotted the "One Stop Shop" up ahead that housed both the station and the city council offices and jogged across the quiet street. My stomach tightened with nerves, but I squared my shoulders and marched in. I didn't like the idea of leading DI Prescott on, and I'd do my best to avoid it, but I had to try to protect Gus and Fitz.

I didn't much care if that pompous Darius, Fitz's vampire sire and head of the council, got chased off by some cloves of garlic, though. At least I had a good excuse for coming to see Prescott—I needed to pass along that little tidbit Ariel had dropped last night.

I waited my turn in the short line within the bare bones lobby, and finally made it up to the officer behind the reception desk.

"I'm here to see DI Prescott."

She raised a brow. "Do you have an appointment?"

I shook my head.

"Sign in." She slid a clipboard and pen to me. "I'll let him know he has a visitor."

I wrote my name, date, and time of arrival down. Under "reason for visit" I hesitated, then went with "sharing evidence." That sounded businesslike—not at all like I was showing up at his work to flirt.

I waited for a few minutes on a hard plastic chair, then the woman at the desk waved me back up. She pointed at the door to my left. "Head down the hall, make your first left, and then it'll be that big door at the end."

I nodded, and the door buzzed, then clicked unlocked. I followed her directions, my boots clicking along the scuffed linoleum as I passed a few uniformed officers and a man in a suit with an ID badge clipped to his lapel. Metal doors with security scanners lined the hall, but I soon found the one the officer had indicated. I peeked through a narrow security glass window and waved as DI Prescott walked up.

He gave a wan grin in return, and then I stepped back as he buzzed me in and opened the door for me.

Prescott stood to the side. "Minnie! I apologize, I've been meaning to check in—how are you?"

"Fine, thanks." I frowned as I stepped in past him. Better than I could say for him. His shirt and tie were wrinkled, thick stubble covered his chin and cheeks, and the bags under his eyes made me suspect he hadn't slept last night.

"This way?" He led me across the large room over to his desk, one in a long row of them, though none of the nearby workstations were currently occupied. Men and women bustled about, files in hand or chatting in small groups. It looked like any other office, except for all the badges pinned to chests.

"Have a seat."

I took the battered chair across from him, and he settled back in at his desk. My eyes widened at the massive stack of file folders and papers in his to-do box, the case files and the various mugs stained with coffee rings. My gaze lingered on a scrap of paper in an evidence bag.

It read:

I know about you and the Italian. I'll tell him unless you pay up. I want £15,000! If you don't—

I startled as Prescott grabbed the note and stuffed it into a drawer.

Guess I wasn't supposed to see that.

He let out a dry chuckle. "Life's been a little crazy lately. Probably need to tidy up." He raked a hand through his thick, kinky hair. Poor guy. What was going on that had him so ragged?

"So, what brings you by?" He waved a hand. "I mean—not that I'm not delighted to see you, I am."

I shot him a smile. "Well, I ran into Ariel Morgenstern last night. The gal who works as a prop master at the theater."

He raised his brows. "Where did you see her?"

"Uh—" I couldn't exactly tell him it'd been at a witch's meeting. Mim had warned me against telling many people the truth about my powers. Not that she needed to—I'd learned the lesson firsthand when I'd told Desmond, only for him to throw it back in my face.

I shook that terrible memory off. "At a pub." It wasn't a lie... I was just leaving out the Equinox celebration bit.

He nodded for me to go on.

"She recognized me from the other night at the theater and asked me to pass something along to you. She said you should look into Richard."

He cocked his head. "The director."

I nodded. "She said he was quite possessive of Petra." I bit my lip. "I'm not sure why that would lead him to commit murder, but I thought it best to pass it along to you anyway."

Prescott leaned back in his chair and crossed an ankle over one knee. "Interesting." He nibbled on a pen. "Unfortunately, Richard's got an airtight alibi. He was mingling with the audience and has witnesses who saw him from the moment the curtain came down to the moment her body was discovered."

"Oh, right." I myself had seen him in the lobby and even been with him that awful moment in Petra's dressing room.

Prescott shook his head, his gaze far away. "Coroner said the victim must've been killed mere minutes, maybe even seconds, before she was discovered."

How terrible. To think, if Harvey or anyone had just checked on her sooner, Petra might still be alive. I cleared my throat, looking for an angle to get information about the possible vampire hunter. "I'm sorry that wasn't more helpful. How's the case coming along?"

That seemed to jolt him out of his reverie. He sat

forward and leaned his elbows on an open file folder. "It's coming along. Not as quickly as I'd like, but..." He shrugged. "We're doing our best, and I appreciate you coming by to tell me about that." He planted his palms and scooted back, as if he was about to rise and show me out. "Anything else? I apologize, but I'm terribly busy."

Yes! I needed to know if he was hanging out with a vampire hunter. "Uh—well..." I fumbled for an excuse to keep talking. "Is it that other case that's got you so busy? The one that involves that man in the trench coat?"

His eyes narrowed with suspicion, and a muscle in his jaw jumped. "That's one of them, yes."

I'd definitely struck a nerve with that question, but it seemed to have only shut him down. I sucked in a deep breath and tried another angle.

I forced a light laugh. "I know this'll sound nuts, but I thought I overhead the two of you talking about vampires, of all things!"

I wanted so badly for him to laugh it off. Instead, his dark complexion turned ashen, and his dark eyes widened. Uh-oh. That's *exactly* what they'd been talking about.

He let out a humorless chuckle, his lip curled. "That is crazy. I'm sorry, Minnie, but I really must be getting back to work."

He rose and I was forced to the same. *Snakes.* He was practically chasing me away. My stomach turned. That only seemed to confirm that he and that strange man knew more about vampires than he wanted to let on. This was not good news.

He nodded toward the door I'd entered and escorted me toward it.

"Uh... you know, it's too bad our date got cut short." Oof, I felt terrible for leading him on. "Maybe we can, uh, spend some more time together soon. I'd love to get to know you better... your hobbies..." If they include vampire hunting...

"Uh, sure." Prescott seemed distracted, like his over-worked mind was already back to being consumed with whatever this mysterious case was.

I tried for a bright smile. "Oh, great. Maybe tonight?"

He frowned. "Oh... I'm attending the play again tonight, to do some more investigating."

We both startled when the door to the hallway flew open and a handsome, middle-aged man in a sharp suit entered, flanked by a smaller man in glasses and the officer from the reception desk.

The officer looked relieved. "Oh good, Prescott. I was hoping to catch you. This gentleman says he has information about the theater case."

I looked between Prescott and the guy in the nice suit, intrigued.

Prescott frowned. "Who are you?"

The dark-haired guy glanced at the man with the brief-case beside him, who nodded. The tall guy stepped forward and smoothed back his dark hair, gray at the temples, then adjusted his lapels.

"Officer." His deep voice dripped with a heavy Italian accent. "I am Petra Cornflower's husband."

11

THE SECRET

Petra's husband? I gaped. But the night she'd been murdered, Ariel and Richard had vouched that she was single—not even seeing anyone.

Prescott shook his head. "We were unaware Petra was married."

The guy splayed his large, tanned hands. "It was a big secret."

Prescott studied the guy for a long moment, then turned to the officer who'd escorted him in. "Please let DI O'Brien know about the situation."

She nodded and walked briskly off across the room.

Wow. A secret marriage—just like in *Emma*! I couldn't help my curiosity. I'd been among the group who'd discovered Petra's body, after all, and now this shocking bombshell?

The man with the briefcase stepped forward and shook Prescott's hand. "I'm Mr. Rossi's attorney."

Prescott turned to me. "Sorry, Minnie, please excuse me."

I waved him off. "Of course."

The men wandered back to Prescott's desk, and I lingered, torn between getting information and being polite. Prescott had obviously been dismissing me, and hanging around now would border on pushiness. At the same time, I'd come this far and didn't want to return empty-handed to Gus and Fitz. Maybe if I hung around, I'd get another shot at working some information out of Prescott about that guy in the trench coat. That, and I couldn't help but feel curious about this secret husband.

I meandered nearer and lingered behind the water cooler. I slowly plucked a paper cup off the stack and took my time filling it up, darting glances at the group gathered around Prescott's desk. DI O'Brien, all scowls and business, marched over and pulled up a chair.

The older cop narrowed his eyes at the Italian guy. "No one we've spoken to was aware Petra was married. Where's your proof?"

The lawyer pulled a document out of his briefcase and handed it to O'Brien. "Their marriage certificate."

Prescott and O'Brien bent their heads together and pored over it while I took a sip of water and watched them out of the corner of my eye.

O'Brien's forehead wrinkled, and he glanced up at the Italian guy, Mr. Rossi. "This is dated three weeks ago." He arched a bushy brow. "You're newlyweds."

Mr. Rossi nodded.

O'Brien glared at him. "The roses in her dressing room. Those from you?"

Again, he nodded.

Prescott pulled his lips to the side. "Why'd you keep it a secret?"

I watched the Italian's back. He shrugged. "It was Petra's idea. That director, he was so possessive of her."

I frowned. That was exactly how Ariel had put it last night.

Rossi splayed his hands. "She was planning to retire from acting and travel the world with me. She wanted one last performance on the stage. This run of *Emma* was to be her last."

How sad. And in a different way than she'd intended, it had been.

A new marriage, a secret husband, and possessive director? My witchy intuition told me to pay attention, that this likely had something to do with Petra's murder.

Prescott shook his head. "Help me understand. You say Richard was possessive. Did Petra think her career would be affected if he knew you two were married?"

The Italian guy nodded. "Exactly. Richard felt like he owned Petra, like he was the reason for her success. He would yell at her if another man, even a stagehand or another actor, talked to her outside of rehearsing. He was controlling and would have been angry if he'd known we were together."

O'Brien glared at him, his gravelly voice dripping with suspicion. "And yet, you said she was retiring. So why would she care?"

Mr. Rossi scoffed and threw a hand up. "Richard could still get to her. My Petra was afraid Richard would pull her from the lead part early." He shook a finger at the detectives. "Petra generated much jealousy, you know. Her rival was very eager for her part."

I bit my lip. Her rival? Could he be talking about the actress who'd played her rival on stage as well, Elinor? At the tearoom, Calvin had mentioned the play was still going on. If Elinor was now playing the lead part, that boost to her career gave her motive to kill Petra. Especially if Richard was as obsessed with Petra as her husband and Ariel had made it seem. Maybe Elinor felt that taking Petra out of the picture was the only way to get the director to notice her.

Prescott nodded. "Petra was young. What was her plan after retirement?"

Mr. Rossi leaned back in his chair and splayed his hands. "I'm rich. I was going to support her."

O'Brien glared at him. "How romantic. Where were you the night she was killed?"

Mr. Rossi scoffed. "I was at the theater, of course. Supporting my wife."

The detective inspectors exchange significant looks.

Prescott pressed his lips together. "Why wait till now to come forward?"

Good question. Especially since he'd been present at the theater the night Petra was killed. Surely he'd been interviewed by the police then. He must've lied to them, at least by omission. If the whole point of the deception had been to keep Richard from punishing Petra, what could he have stood to gain by keeping the secret after her death?

Mr. Rossi turned to his lawyer, who nodded for him to go on.

The Italian guy shook his head. "I'm not born yesterday, Detective Inspectors. I know how it goes in real life. It's always the husband, right? I knew it wouldn't look good, and I admit I panicked a bit. I wanted to get my lawyer in place and take care of myself, first."

He had a point, yet it still seemed odd that his new bride would be murdered, and his first thought would be to protect himself. Then again, I'd never been in his shoes.

Prescott and O'Brien bent their heads together again and exchanged a few quiet words, then O'Brien held up a plastic bag with a paper inside and slid it over to Mr. Rossi.

"Have you seen this before?"

I sucked in a breath. That must be the note in the evidence bag I'd seen on Prescott's desk earlier. The one demanding £15,000 to keep "the Italian" secret from "him." Mr. Rossi had to be the Italian, which made it likely that the director, Richard, was the "him."

Mr. Rossi nodded. "Some idiot left that for Petra under her dressing room door."

O'Brien narrowed his dark, sparkling eyes. "So your marriage wasn't a complete secret. Someone was black-mailing Petra."

Mr. Rossi nodded.

Prescott leaned forward. "Any idea who sent that?"

Mr. Rossi shook his head. "Petra and I talked it over. She said she'd told a few crew members about us, but she didn't think they'd have threatened her. Could've been anyone—well, anyone on the production who knew about the dynamic between her and Richard."

"And you two didn't think to contact the police about this?"

Petra's husband shrugged. "I wish we had, now. But Petra knew it meant the secret would get out. Plus, she thought it was just a bluff. She said we should just ignore it."

Prescott massaged the bridge of his nose. "Do you know which people Petra told about your marriage?"

He shook his head. "She just said a couple close people she could trust."

"Excuse me."

I jumped at the sound of someone right behind me, then whirled to find a guy in a suit with his brows raised. He held up a stainless steel water bottle, then glanced at the water cooler, which I was totally blocking.

"Oh—sorry."

I stepped aside, and Prescott looked up. We made eye contact, and I gave a sheepish grin.

"Minnie? You're still here? Sorry, did you need something?"

Er... besides eavesdropping? I walked a few steps closer, and all the men looked up at me. "I just wanted to finish our conversation, but how about I meet you tonight at the theater? We can continue our talk there." That would give me a chance to pester him without a time limit.

He frowned. "Uh... I'll be working."

I purposely misunderstood him. "I don't mind." I wiggled my fingers in a wave. "See you then!" I sped out of there, my cheeks burning with embarrassment. Prescott probably thought I was crazy into him... or just crazy. I sure hoped Gus and Fitz appreciated my efforts to keep them safe.

12

GOSSIP

I headed into work, where Fitz warned me off my plan to tag along with Prescott at the theater. I imagined his concern came from a mix of worry about my safety and apprehension about me cozying up to DI Prescott. After putting in several hours of marketing efforts, I scooped up my cat and walked home to change.

I put on my green, long-sleeved velvet cocktail dress and heels, petted Tilda (who was curled up sleeping on my bed), and then carefully went down the steep, polished staircase. Gus, hair mussed from sleeping all day, poked his head out of his room. When I told him my plan, he thanked me for being a stalker.

I was unenthusiastic and embarrassed over my clingy behavior when I walked up to the Theatre Royal. A small crowd in dresses and dinner jackets filed in through the three arched doorways, which were topped with a gold royal coat of arms. I gulped and steeled myself to act chipper, despite wishing I was back at Gus's in my sweats with my enormous copy of all Jane Austen's works. My heels clicked along the cobblestones as I joined the other theatergoers and filed inside.

When the usher asked for my ticket, I panicked, until I spotted DI Prescott standing in the lobby. He flashed his badge and told the usher I was with him.

"Hey. Thanks for that."

"Don't mention it." He gave me a boyish grin. It reminded me of the way he normally acted, before all the secrecy and bags under the eyes. "You look really great, by the way."

Heat rushed to my cheeks. Maybe this wouldn't be such a bad night after all. "Thanks. You too."

He grinned. "I wasn't totally sure you'd show up." He winced. "Like I said—I've got to work. I'm planning to head backstage and ask around."

I shrugged. "That's all right by me. I don't mind tagging along." I grinned. "I've already seen the play anyway."

Hopefully tonight wouldn't end with another dead actress.

He chuckled. "True enough. But... maybe we'll have time for a drink after?"

I pressed my lips together and gave a little nod, then followed Prescott through a side door that led down a dark hallway. When he pushed through another door at the far end, I recognized that we were backstage.

Unlike the luxurious and serene front of house—all burgundy velvet upholstery, draped curtains, and glittering chandeliers—backstage was raw, practical, and bursting with energy. Several stagehands hurried by, lugging a towering backdrop painted to look like a Regency-era home. I recognized it as Emma's sitting room, complete with a fire in the hearth. A woman pushed a stuffed rack of costumes, and actresses in old-fashioned dresses strolled by, eyes glued to their cell phones.

I glanced at Prescott. Judging by his wide eyes, he seemed just as disoriented as I was. It was dark, crowded, and hectic back here.

I nudged him, and he jumped. "So... where are you going to start?"

That seemed to snap him back to the present. He cleared his throat and pulled out his cellphone. He scanned through some screens of notes, then glanced up. "I'm looking for the director, Richard London."

I nodded and scanned the huge space, crowded with scaffolding, ladders, equipment, and workers. "He might be in the wings? You know, to give cues."

He nodded. "Good thought."

I hurried along beside Prescott's long strides. Suddenly he stopped and peered into the dim light. "Excuse me a moment. I've spotted someone else I'd like to question."

I nodded as he headed toward a small group of stage-hands. I crossed my arms. Guess I'd just wait here.

"You think?"

"I bet it was her, too."

The voices piqued my curiosity. I glanced through a bright doorway to my right. Two women and a young man, all in costume, sat at a long row of mirrors surrounded by globe lights. The ladies sat in chairs, while the young man perched on the counter in front of them, sandwiched between makeup bags and curling irons. I edged closer to the doorway and leaned against it. This must be the communal dressing room.

The young man scoffed. "Think about it. Elinor and Petra were constantly bickering." He rolled his eyes, then pivoted to face the mirror. He penciled in a little more liner under his eyes.

A blond gal bounced her foot. "I don't know. You really think their rivalry was so heated she'd kill over it?"

The other gal snorted and twirled a red ringlet. I recognized her as the actress who played the self-important Mrs. Elton. "Elinor's always been jealous of the way Richard favored Petra. If Elinor did kill her, it kinda worked out perfectly in her favor. I mean, now she's playing the lead and she's Richard's new favorite. And we all know how well-connected Richard is in the theater community. If this was Elinor's way of moving on to bigger and better, brava!"

The blond recoiled. "I can't believe that."

The guy rounded on her. "Did Elinor seem even remotely upset to you? She's happy Petra's gone."

The redhead nodded, her ringlets bouncing. "Show business is cutthroat."

I leaned away from the doorway. *Gee, I guess.* Who knew the drama and politics happening backstage were just as entertaining as the performances on stage? Could these young actors be right? Did Elinor kill Petra, literally stab her in the back, to get the lead and climb her way to the top?

Petra was about to retire. So why kill her if she just had to wait a few weeks? Then again, I doubted Elinor was one of the confidants Petra shared that news with. If Elinor had killed Petra, it was a waste in so many ways. She'd have had her chance in the spotlight if she'd just waited until this run of *Emma* was over.

I frowned. Didn't Elinor have an alibi, though? She'd been in the lobby immediately after the play... but she'd also claimed she was going to leave the meet the cast party early, since Petra wasn't there. It would've been tight, but she might have slipped backstage and killed Petra, then rushed off right before we showed up with Richard for the "back-stage tour."

It might've just been some baseless gossip I'd overheard, but I made a mental note to pass it along to DI Prescott in case it helped. I frowned and glanced around the enormous backstage area. The small group of stagehands had broken up, and the detective inspector was nowhere to be seen. I wandered through the dark, chaotic backstage to find him.

13

THE DIRECTOR

I meandered behind the enormous plywood backdrop, carefully picking my way around piles of cables, until I heard familiar voices.

"Marriage? What? I had no idea."

I crept around a heavy curtain and found Prescott standing with folded arms in front of the director, Richard. Richard pressed a hand dramatically to his blue button-up, the other hand covering his mouthpiece. I raised a brow. The hand against his chest was wrapped in white gauze. Had he injured it?

The hairs rose on the back of my neck, and I had the sensation of someone standing behind me. I glanced back. Bertram Kensington, who played the annoying Mr. Elton, lingered nearby and shot the director a somewhat sinister look. He jumped when he caught me staring, then stalked off. *Creepy.*

Prescott shifted on his feet. "Why did Petra keep the marriage a secret?"

Richard scoffed. "I haven't the foggiest! Maybe it made it more lurid to sneak around?"

Prescott narrowed his eyes. "We've been told you were possessive, controlling even, of Petra. Witnesses have said she was afraid you might punish her if you found out."

Richard gaped. "That's outrageous! Petra was my muse! Of course we were close, and of course I felt protective of her—she starred in countless productions I directed over the years. But Petra was free to do as she pleased." His expression darkened. "Even if she made choices that threatened to ruin her career."

A young woman dressed all in black rushed up to Richard, a clipboard hugged to her chest. She ignored Prescott. "There you are! Why aren't you answering? Is your mic working? We've got an issue in wardrobe."

Richard shot Prescott an exaggerated, apologetic look. "I'd love to chat more, Detective Inspector, but it's a busy night." He flashed his eyes. "I'm directing a play."

Prescott frowned. "I noticed. Isn't it a little cold to continue with the production?"

The gal with the clipboard shook her head at Prescott, and Richard shrugged. "As they say, the show must go on!" He turned to walk off with the gal, who was urgently beckoning him to follow, but paused and spun to face DI Prescott again. "Oh. But I did remember something." He stepped closer, and Prescott bent forward. "The night poor Petra was killed, I overheard a rather heated argument between her and Harvey Smythe, the young man who plays Mr. Knightley?"

Prescott nodded for him to continue.

"Well, I was under the impression they were friends, but it certainly didn't sound like it that night."

Prescott narrowed his dark eyes. "And you're just *now* remembering this?"

Richard twirled his bandaged hand. "It was a whirlwind

of a night, Detective. It only came to me later." He shook a finger. "Don't go interrogating my actors now, promise me. They need to focus on their performances."

Prescott scoffed. "This is a police investigation. It takes priority."

I stepped forward. "Excuse me, but—what happened to your hand?" It'd looked fine the night before.

Richard rolled his eyes. "Clumsy me. I burned it on a hot pan."

The director at last followed his nearly panicked assistant, and I slid up beside Prescott.

He pressed his lips together. "Sorry I wandered off. I spotted Richard, and as you probably saw, he's a difficult man to pin down."

I nodded. "No worries." We watched the director as he sped through the maze of scaffolding, workers, and set pieces.

Prescott let out a heavy sigh. "You know, I always used to think my partner, O'Brien, was just an old grump, but the longer I do this job, the more I'm afraid I'm turning into him."

I chuckled. "You're still the nice cop, don't worry. And you've got more charm in your little finger than O'Brien probably ever had."

This got a little grin out of him. "Thanks."

I rocked on my heels. "Guess you're going to be having a word with that actor, Harvey Smythe, next?"

He grinned down at me. "You're turning into a regular detective yourself."

I gave him a playful salute. "Since you're missing a partner tonight, how about I help out and play bad cop?"

This got an actual laugh out of him. "No offense, Minnie,

but I don't think you could scare anyone, no matter how hard you tried. And I mean that as a compliment."

I thought of the way Fitz had frightened off my ex the other day. Maybe I personally wasn't the scariest, but I had friends who could be pretty intimidating.

"But I do think it's a good idea if you stick close to me from here on out." He peered into the dimly lit expanse behind the stage. "It's dark, and who knows who's lurking back here."

I lowered my voice to a whisper. "So you suspect Petra's killer is a member of the cast or crew?"

He cleared his throat. "Er, yes, possibly."

I frowned as I started off after him. If he wasn't talking about Petra's killer, then what dangerous person did he imagine might be lurking in the shadows? Was he referring to vampires? My heels clicked on the concrete floor as I jogged along after him.

And while I had to agree with Prescott that I probably wouldn't make the best bad cop, I wasn't so sure he was right about the scaring people part. I had magic coursing through my veins, and I had a feeling if Prescott ever got a glimpse of the magic I was capable of, it'd probably freak him right out. My stomach sank as I realized it was just another reason he and I weren't the best match.

I'd gone through my whole marriage keeping my witchy abilities (novice as they were) secret from my now ex. And once I'd caved and told him the truth, he'd thrown it back in my face. No—I wouldn't ever live a lie again, not with a partner. I wanted to be able to be myself—my whole self—around the people closest to me.

14

HARVEY

After a few minutes of asking around, Prescott and I found his suspect waiting in the wings.

"Harvey Smythe?"

The tall young man, who'd been peering past the velvet curtains to watch the action on stage, startled and whirled to face us. His wide eyes softened, and he pressed a hand to his heart. "Sorry." He spoke in a hushed voice. "You startled me. Can I help you?" He winced and thumbed toward the stage. "I'm about to go on."

Prescott stepped forward. "We'll make this quick."

Harvey's dark, drawn-in brows pinched together as he spotted the badge pinned to Prescott's lapel, the stage makeup exaggerating his expression.

"Did you and Petra Cornflower have an argument the night she was killed?"

Harvey paled. "Er…" He plastered on a smile that didn't quite reach his eyes. "It was just a little disagreement."

Judging by his reaction, I suspected it was something more serious.

Prescott raised a brow. "About?"

Harvey's eyes darted about. "Uh..." He scoffed. "She... was going to get a cat, but I was like no, girl! Are you crazy? You're so allergic!"

He leaned forward and raised his brows high. "I mean, one whiff of cat and she'd be sneezing and coughing all night. She was kind of a diva about it. If someone came to rehearsal and smelled like cat, she'd complain, and Richard would make them go home and change. And once she got triggered, she'd have to take antihistamines, which made her crazy drowsy. I mean, that's what happened the night she..." He gulped and dropped his gaze. "You know."

I cocked my head. "*What* happened, exactly?"

Prescott raised his brows at me.

Oops. Probably overstepping my bounds. Maybe he was right—I was turning into an amateur sleuth.

Harvey blinked. "She had a reaction, obviously."

"To?"

He raised his brows. "*Somehow,* the *inside* of her costume got covered in cat hair."

Prescott frowned. "Odd." He pulled his phone out and typed in some notes.

Harvey scoffed. "More than odd. Someone planted it there, knowing it'd trigger her allergies. And I can bet who."

Prescott raised a brow.

Harvey leaned forward, clearly enjoying having juicy gossip to share. "Elinor. It's just the kind of backhanded prank she'd pull, too."

Interesting. If Elinor and Petra were rivals, the actress seemed like the logical culprit. But was it more than a prank? Had that sabotage somehow led to Petra's death?

Harvey returned to watching the stage.

"How dreadful for poor Mrs. Weston," the actor playing Emma's father droned on.

Harvey turned back to us. "Anyway, that night Petra had hives and was coughing and sneezing. She could barely get through her lines, so between me and Ariel—that's the prop master—we scrounged up like four antihistamines for her." He scoffed. "Two would normally knock her out. I was surprised Petra didn't pass out onstage." The color drained from his face. "Oh my gosh, but she *did* die!" He gasped. "Do you think it was an overdose?" He covered his mouth with both hands, his eyes wide.

Prescott took a deep breath. "No. She was stabbed in the back."

Harvey's shoulders dropped down. "Oh. Right." He darted a look at the stage. "I'm sorry, but I've really got to go. I'm about to make my big entrance."

I frowned. I believed him about the cat hair in Petra's dress, but if she was that extremely allergic, why would she have been thinking about getting a cat? The reason for their argument didn't track.

He stepped away from us, but I darted forward and caught the sleeve of his jacket. "Wait! Did you know about Petra's secret marriage?"

He whirled, his eyes wide. "You know about that?"

Prescott raised his brows. "You too, apparently?"

Harvey whimpered. "Okay, yes. Yes!" he hissed. "That's what we were *really* arguing about. I didn't like her husband, okay? I told her she'd regret it, and now she's dead!" He grimaced. "It was him!"

Prescott blinked. "Her husband? Mr. Rossi?"

Harvey nodded emphatically. "And I'm probably next for telling you this!"

I tilted my head. "Why didn't you like her husband, and what makes you think he killed her?"

Harvey sniffed. "Well, for one, he seemed shady. He has

gobs of money and from *what* exactly? He only told her 'various holdings.'" He made air quotes. "Mmkay, sure. And he was like twenty years older than Petra—she was settling." He held a hand to the side of his mouth. "And frankly, she's always been more into the *ladies* than the fellas. I knew she wouldn't be happy—not in the long run. Plus, giving up acting? She'd regret it! And if you need more reasons, she told me they'd been fighting a lot lately and she was already having doubts. Apparently, he was pressuring her to sign a prenup... *after* they'd already been married!"

I raised a brow. That was certainly a different picture than the one of newlywedded bliss her husband had painted this morning down at the station.

"I SAID—I do believe that's Mr. Knightley at the door!"

Harvey's eyes widened. "That's my cue!" He dashed onstage, forcing his face into an exaggerated smile.

"Emma, Mr. Woodhouse. How good to see you this evening."

15

VAMPIRE BUSINESS

Prescott and I moved away from the stage, further into the shadows.

"I'll have to have another word with Mr. Rossi." He tapped more notes into his phone.

I nodded. "He had good reason to fear suspicion being thrown on him."

Prescott shot me a curious look, and my cheeks flushed hot.

"Sorry. I couldn't help but overhear." From where I was hiding behind the water cooler...

He cleared his throat and spoke in a flat tone. "No worries." He tucked his phone back into his jacket pocket. "Listen, Minnie, I've got a lot more work to do, it seems. I was hoping this would be fairly routine, but I'm not sure I'll have much time to spend with you and—"

My mind whirled. I could see where this was going, and no way was I going to have gotten all dressed up and made excuses to tail Prescott yet again without getting any answers about the mysterious man in the trench coat.

"Do you believe in ghosts?" I blurted it out, half-surprising myself.

Prescott cleared his throat. "Uh... what?"

"Ghosts." I lifted a palm. "Yeah, I uh—I have a friend who thinks she's being haunted."

He let out a weary sigh. "You know, until recently I'd have laughed at something like that. I'd have said there must be a scientific explanation or suspected your friend might be suffering from some mental health issues." He shook his head. "Now I have reason to believe in the supernatural."

My eyes widened. That was not what I was hoping to hear. It seemed only to confirm my fears that Prescott knew about the existence of vampires.

I took a shaky breath. "Well, if you *do* believe... what do you think my friend should do? Maybe try to find out what the ghost wants? Or have a seance to communicate with it and help it to move on towards the light?"

His expression darkened. "I'd tell your friend that supernatural entities are dangerous and not to be trifled with. She should probably move if she can."

I gulped, my pulse quickening.

"It's my job to protect good people from monsters—whether they be human or paranormal—and if I knew how to destroy that ghost, I'd do it."

The word "monsters" stung. Of course, Prescott had no idea he was speaking to a witch—a supernatural being right in front of him. But he'd just told me that presented with something paranormal, he'd deem it a monster and try to destroy it.

I inched back, and he frowned. "Sorry, Minnie. Did I say something?"

I shook my head. "Nope!"

He looked down and licked his lips. "Listen, I'm really sorry for the last few days." He scrubbed his scruffy chin. "I think you're a great girl, and I'd really love to see where this could go, but my life lately has gotten... complicated."

He pressed his lips into a tight smile. "And though I appreciate your interest and effort to make this work around my professional life"—he gestured around us—"I just—I don't have the bandwidth, right now, to get involved with anyone." He winced. "Again, I'm really sorry."

I felt mixed emotions. On one hand, I'd been so afraid of leading him on that I was both relieved and a little amused that he was the one breaking it off. On the other hand, it stung my pride, just a little, to have him thinking I probably couldn't take a hint. That, and I was now almost convinced he knew about vampires—not good—and even worse, viewed anything supernatural as a threat to be taken out.

I plastered on a manic smile and thumbed over my shoulder. "Um, that's totally fine. I understand. I'll just, uh, head home."

He stepped toward me, his hand outstretched. "Let me walk you back, at least. It's not safe out there."

My throat tightened. I *didn't* feel safe... from him! He'd already walked me home once, but I had no intention of leading him right to the doorstep of my best friend in the world, who just happened to be a vampire.

I shook my head. "No, that's okay. I'm right around the corner, and it's not even late."

Before he could insist, I whirled and dashed off toward the exit, my heels clicking on the hard floors. My mind racing, I walked the chilly streets of Bath back to Gus's.

Couples strolled by hand in hand, and an older man walked a small dog. Bright light spilled from the windows of the shops and restaurants I passed. It was just another night in gorgeous Bath, but suddenly every dark alleyway and shadowed doorstep seemed ominous and threatening.

Ironically, my fear didn't come from the vampires who I knew crawled the city, but from the detective I'd just gone on a date with and whatever vampire hunter I was now convinced he was working with. I was out of breath by the time I jogged up the steps to Gus's front door and threw myself inside, locking it tight behind me.

"Gus?"

No answer came. My vampire roommate must be out—I hoped he was safe.

I stepped out of my heels, threw off my coat, and tromped upstairs to my attic room. I tried to quiet my anxious thoughts by reading from my beloved collection of Jane Austen's works—a little *Sense and Sensibility* seemed just the thing. I snuggled up on my bedspread with Tilda and escaped the worries of reality for a bit with a good book.

I must've dozed off, because the next thing I knew, my cheek was stuck to the pages. I yawned and patted around for my phone to check the time—it was now after eleven. I'd been asleep for hours! I pushed upright, and Tilda rose as well, arching her back in a big stretch. I frowned at the muffled sound of voices. Gus must be back—and he had someone with him.

Still in my velvet green dress and stockings, I padded downstairs with Tilda in my arms.

"Minnie?"

Fitz sat with Gus beside the fire. My boss immediately rose to his feet (as he did anytime a lady entered the room) and held his arms stiff at his sides, his brow pinched with concern.

"Good evening."

"Hi." I grinned, and the knot of worry in my chest relaxed a little. Gus and Fitz were both here, safe from the vampire hunter... for now.

Fitz waited until I flopped down on the chaise beside Gus before he sat in the armchair opposite us. His dark eyes stayed glued to my face.

Gus lifted a blond brow. "So... how'd it go?"

"Prescott told me he didn't *used* to believe in supernatural creatures, but now does, and would destroy any 'monster' he happened across." I flashed my eyes at Gus and Fitz as I scratched Tilda's chest. "I think that puts all three of us in danger."

Tilda meowed.

I nuzzled my cheek against her. "Not you, you cute little thing. No one would think *you* were a monster."

Gus groaned. "How bothersome."

Fitz shot him a hard look. "A bit more than bothersome, I should say. I agree, Minnie. This seems to confirm that Prescott is not only aware of supernatural creatures but views them as threats."

Gus sipped from his wine glass of blood. "Gee. I wonder where he got such an idea?"

I sighed. "The vampire hunter?"

They both nodded.

I slumped lower in my seat. "Great. What do we do now?"

"We'll handle it." Fitz shot me a significant look. "You don't need to get any more involved."

Gus tipped his glass back and polished off the last of its red contents, then pushed to his feet. "And *right* now, we have an errand to run."

Gus was dressed to go out in black skinny jeans and a black sweater.

"Where are you going?"

Gus winked at me. "Vampire business."

That was the answer he always gave me when he meant

he wasn't going to tell me. Vampires and their secrecy—so annoying.

Fitz rose as well, still decked out in his butler getup with coattails and shiny black brogues. "I'm not sure that's still the wisest idea, given what Minnie just told us."

Gus shrugged as he carried his empty glass to the gorgeous state-of-the-art kitchen. "I agree. But we don't have much choice. My fridge is empty."

Fitz huffed. "Mine too."

I raised a brow. Somehow, I couldn't imagine Fitz having a fridge. I'd never been to his home, but Gus had mentioned that he owned a sprawling estate that left him cash poor. And Fitz himself had told me he wasn't the best about upkeep. I imagined some half-crumbling mansion, surrounded by dark and twisty woods. Just the kind of home for a vampire... with no place for something as modern as a fridge.

Gus strolled back out of the kitchen and headed for the coat rack by the front door. "We're headed to the blood bank."

I scooted forward. "I'll go with." Tilda meowed as if to say she wanted to tag along too.

Fitz folded his thick arms. "No. It's too dangerous."

Gus rolled his eyes. "She'll be fine."

I grinned and shot to my feet. This was the first time, aside from the vampire council meeting, that I'd been allowed to tag along on "vampire business."

Gus shot Tilda a flat look. "I suppose the cat is coming too?"

I grinned. "You know we can't stop her if she puts her mind to it."

Fitz shot me a side-eye look. "Reminds me of someone."

16

BLOOD

A light rain fell as Gus, Fitz, Tilda, and I came to a stop. We stood across the slick cobblestone street from the vampire blood bank in a not-so-great part of Bath. Cracks marred the walls of buildings, some tagged with graffiti, and trash piled high in the alleys.

I shot Fitz a grateful smile as he held his wood-handled umbrella over my head, letting small droplets cling to his own wavy head of hair. Always the gentleman. He grinned down at me, tenderness in his eyes.

Gus cleared his throat, and we both jumped. My friend jerked his chin at the nondescript, three-story stone building across the way. "Ready?" The front windows were all dark, but a light shone from a basement window tucked around the side.

I smirked. "Two vampires, a witch and a familiar walk into a blood bar—"

"Bank," Gus corrected me as we jogged across the street.

I raised a brow. "So it's just for vampires? How does that work?"

"It's vampire-run." Fitz tilted his head. "And donors are

well compensated for their contributions. It allows us vampires to survive without preying on humans. It benefits all."

I frowned. "Do all vampires get their, uh, meals from the bank?"

Fitz's expression darkened. "Not all."

I had a feeling he might be referring to the council and his sire, Darius. He seemed like just the kind of creep to lurk in dark alleyways, pouncing on the unsuspecting.

We walked down a narrow side yard overgrown with weeds and thick bushes. A few stone steps led down to a door with no sign—just a barred, frosted window lit from within.

Gus jogged down the steps, his shoes scuffing along the rough stone. Just as he reached out to grab the handle, the door flung open and an odd-looking man shoved out. He edged around Gus, giving me a good look at his face in the light spilling from the door.

It was the actor who played Mr. Elton in the play—Bertram Kensington—and he was still wearing his stage makeup from the performance earlier this evening. I gasped, and Fitz edged in between me and the man as Tilda arched her back and hissed.

"It's okay," I whispered.

We all held still, tensed, until he shuffled off into the night. Gus and Fitz shot me questioning looks.

I huddled close with them. "That was one of the actors from the play. What was he doing here?"

"I got a big whiff—he wasn't a vampire. I'd guess he was donating blood." Gus crinkled his nose. "And he needed a shower."

Fitz gazed in the direction Bertram had gone. "He must be low on funds."

I frowned. I supposed being an actor, even for a prestigious theater like the Royal, might not pay a living wage. We continued down the stairs, and I was surprised to find the interior of the blood bank clean and modern, in contrast to the dingy exterior.

A clean-cut young man with pale skin stood behind the counter, while a few men sat reading magazines around the small lobby.

He raised his brows as we approached, lingering for a moment on Tilda before turning back to Gus, Fitz, and me. "Here for a deposit or a purchase?"

"Purchase."

The worker slid a form on a clipboard across the counter to Gus. I peeked over his shoulder as he marked preferences for various blood types. Interesting.

I leaned close to Fitz and whispered, "Do the, uh, donors know this goes to vampires?"

He shook his head. "Absolutely not."

Huh. Something about that struck me as somewhat dishonest. After Gus finished with the form, it was Fitz's turn to order. As Gus came to stand beside me, I whispered out of the corner of my mouth, "So these people think they're selling their blood to go to hospitals and such?"

Gus shrugged. "I suppose so."

I clicked my tongue. "This blood could be helping people who need transfusions."

Gus shot me a pitying look. "Oh, Minnie, please." He jerked his head toward the men waiting behind us. "That's what people *donate* for. This lot is getting paid." He raised his blond brows.

He had a point. "Still. It's not quite up-and-up."

He scoffed. "What about your meals? Do you always

make sure the chicken you order at a restaurant was pasture-raised? Or that you buy organic?"

My cheeks grew hot. "Well... no. But I do my best to be ethical."

He lifted his nose. "We're all just doing our best, too. At least we know the humans who give blood here are paid well. And it's cage free; they have as much room to run around as they want."

I chuckled. "Okay. Fair enough."

He nudged me. "And believe me, it's better than the alternative."

I shuddered at the thought of Darius, head of the vampire council, skulking along in the shadows ready to pounce and drain an unsuspecting victim. "True."

Fitz finished filling out the form, and the young man—who was probably a thousand-year-old vampire who only appeared to be twenty-two—handed them two discreet white paper bags, sealed and quite heavy by the looks of them. That'd probably be a good week's worth of meals for each of them.

Tilda trotted ahead as we climbed back out into the chilly, drizzly dark night and headed back to Gus's. I was about to step around the corner when Fitz lunged forward and caught my shoulder. I spun to face him, and he pressed a finger to his lips. Had they heard something I'd missed?

We all crept quietly forward and peered around the chipped stone building. Across the street and a little way down a dark alley, two shadowy figures faced each other.

I narrowed my eyes, peering into the darkness. "Who is that?"

Gus whispered, "That man who left just before us, the actor."

Bertram? "Who's he talking to?"

Fitz shook his head. "It's unclear, but—"

He and Gus suddenly whipped their heads to look at each other, their eyes wide.

"What?"

Gus bent his head close to mine and whispered in my ear. "The other man is hounding the actor for information. The actor's telling him to pay up or get lost."

Fitz and Gus leapt back and pulled me with them moments before the actor stormed out of the alleyway, muttering and shaking his head. We all pressed close to the side of the building and peeked around the corner. Another man stepped forward, and my eyes widened as I recognized him.

I stifled a gasp. "It's him." I turned from Gus to Fitz.

The man's trench coat fluttered around his ankles as he marched down the street in his military boots. My heart pounded in my chest.

"It's the man I saw speaking to DI Prescott the other night at the theater." I gulped. "The one who said something about vampires."

Icy fear flooded my stomach.

"And now he's loitering outside a vampire blood bank." Gus stepped back and straightened. He shot Fitz a grim look. "At least we've seen him now and can describe him." His throat bobbed. "I'll spread the word."

"No." Fitz bit his lip. "I think we should wait."

Gus scoffed. "For what? For him to stake one of us?" He threw an arm toward the street.

Fitz shook his head, his dark gaze glued to Gus's face. "If the council finds out, that man is as good as dead, which could cause more trouble for us with the humans." He raised his thick brows and darted a glance at me. "Especially if, as Minnie says, he's consorting with the police."

Gus ran a hand through his damp blond hair. "I don't like this." He paced. "You're right. But I don't like it."

I dipped down and scooped Tilda into my arms. I didn't like the idea of my friends being in danger, either.

Fitz looked at me for a long moment, then turned to Gus. "You take Minnie home—be safe. I'll trail the suspected vampire hunter."

My throat grew tight. "Fitz..."

He raised a brow.

I wasn't sure how to express the terror and worry I felt for him... and there was another strong emotion mixed in that I wasn't ready to look at just yet. The best I could come up with was "Be careful."

A small grin tugged at the corner of his mouth. "Always."

17

A THEORY

That night I slept in restless fits. Feeling achy and disheveled, I decided to work from bed in my pj's for the first part of the next day. But eventually, the sun shining in through my attic window called to me, and I dressed in jeans, a white button-up, and my camel coat and carried Tilda through the chilly afternoon streets over to the tearoom.

I was too tired for one of Fitz's scoldings about bringing Tilda through the kitchen, so I stepped in the front door. The bell tinkled, announcing my arrival, and all the butlers looked up from the table they crowded around, folding cloth napkins into fans.

"Minnie!" Calvin waved his whole arm.

I grinned back and crouched to let my squirming cat loose. "Hey, guys."

Tilda, tail in the air, trotted straight over to Leo, her favorite. She meowed, and the stocky guy leaned over to pick her up. She placed her paws on his beefy chest and nuzzled under his chin.

Cho and I exchanged knowing looks. Leo liked to act

tough and macho, but underneath all the muscles and bravado, he was a big softy. As evidenced by the way he cooed over my familiar.

I loosened my coat and walked into the empty dining room. The fire still crackled in the hearth, and clinks and bangs came from the kitchen, where Fitz was no doubt hard at work. Did the guy ever take a day off?

I raised a brow. "Slow one?"

Aldric chuckled, his deep laugh rumbling in his chest. "Hardly. You just caught us at a good time. A little lull before the late afternoon rush."

"Ah." I scratched the back of my neck, my cheeks heating up with embarrassment. I hadn't had a chance yet to address the scene with Desmond the other day.

I turned to Dominik, who fumbled with his napkin. "I wanted to thank you guys for sticking up for me with my ex." I gulped, my throat tight with gratitude. "It meant a lot."

Dom sniffed and pursed his already pouty lips. "That ex of yours was smart to run." He crushed the half-folded napkin into a crumpled ball, the veins in his tattooed neck bulging.

I fought a grin. It was good to have the rough-around-the-edges butler on my side.

Calvin shot me a sympathetic look. "Are you okay? Have you heard any more from him?"

I fiddled with the linen tablecloth. "I'm okay. It shook me up a little, but he hasn't contacted me since, and honestly, I kind of managed to forget about it until now."

I surprised myself with that one. I'd been so upset that day when I marched over to Mim's—and now it was in the back of my mind as I focused on the more pressing issue of the vampire hunter.

Cho shook his head, a charming grin on his tanned face.

"Can you imagine? What a dip! The gall to actually accuse you of being a witch!"

I managed a faltering smile. "Yeah, wild, right?" I looked around this table of young men I considered close friends… practically brothers. I'd never have guessed I could get so close to a group so fast, but they'd welcomed me in with open arms. Would they still stand by me if they knew the truth? Or would they react like Desmond had and hold it against me? Or worse, view me as a dangerous monster like I suspected Prescott would.

I let out a humorless chuckle. "Ha! That'd be crazy, like… if I actually were." I tried to read their reactions. "I mean… a witch wouldn't be *that* bad though, right?"

Leo shot me a puzzled look, and Dominik narrowed his eyes. "What do you mean?"

My mouth went dry just as Fitz poked his head out the swinging door to the kitchen. "Ah, Minnie. I thought I heard your voice. Could you join me? I have a question for you."

Saved by the boss!

I wiggled my fingers in a wave. "See you, guys." I pointed at Leo. "Take good care of my little girl."

He scoffed, then cooed over Tilda. "Oh, please. I spoil you, don't I?" He held a saucer of cream he'd poured for her up to her face to drink.

Cho flashed his eyes at me, and I stifled a laugh as I turned and pushed through to the kitchen. As soon as the door swung open, the heavenly scents of baking bread and hot cranberry scones perfumed the air. I lifted my nose and took a deep inhale, savoring the moment.

When I looked down, I caught Fitz staring at me with those dark eyes, a smile playing at the corner of his mouth.

I lugged my tote bag over and threw it and my coat on a stool. I pulled the other one out and sat across the butcher block workstation from him, resting my elbows on the floury worktop.

"Did you hear me being awkward out there?"

Fitz dipped his face to hide his widening grin as he sliced the crust off finger sandwiches.

I sniffed. "Thought so. Thanks for saving me from myself."

He smiled at me. "I get it. I told you my story, after all." His expression darkened. "When Darius changed me, he forced me to move away from Bath. From all my beloved friends and family."

I gulped. And the woman he'd loved and hoped to court.

He shrugged. "I understand the urge to be accepted and seen for who and what you are." He pressed his lips together and shot me a sympathetic look. "Sometimes I wonder, if Darius hadn't made me move away and I'd told the people I cared about that I'd been made a vampire, if they'd have loved me still."

His gaze grew faraway and then he shook himself. "I'm not sure of the answer, truth be told. Just... be careful, Minnie."

I let out a heavy sigh. "I'm sorry, Fitz, that's really hard." Poor guy. I couldn't imagine losing everyone and everything I cared about in one fell swoop. "And I understand better now the need to be careful who I tell that I'm a witch." I flashed my eyes. "You saw how well it went over with Desmond."

His expression darkened, and his movements with the knife became sharper, quicker.

I moaned. "What am I going to do about him?"

In a flash, Fitz slammed the knife down and looked at me with such intensity it took my breath away. "Did he bother you again?"

I raised my brows. Wow. That was a lot... and pretty hot, if I was honest. I licked my lips. "No. And I doubt he'll come back anytime soon, after you got so..." I twiddled my fingers at my handsome vampire boss as I searched for the right word. "...spooky."

Fitz chuckled, his expression softening. "Spooky?"

I smirked. "Yeah. All the floating and the flickering lights? Spooky."

He grinned and went back to cutting the cucumber sandwiches. "First time I've been called that."

I watched his big hands work for a moment, admiring their strong, graceful movements.

I leaned my cheek into my hand. "Did you learn anything about the guy in the trench coat?"

Fitz shook his head, a loose wavy tendril swishing across his face. "No. He threw me off his trail, which takes skill." He sniffed. "Or I'm just losing my edge, as Gus suggested." His lips pressed together in a grim line. "I'm fairly certain that man is, indeed, a vampire hunter."

A cold wave crashed over me and sent chills up my arms. This guy had managed to lose Fitz, with his supernatural hearing, smell, and speed? I glanced around the normally warm, cozy kitchen and suddenly felt like it was too easy for anyone to walk into. "You should keep the door to the alley locked."

Fitz glanced up at me, a smile in his eyes. "Are you worried about me?"

I shot him a flat look. "Duh."

He chuckled, and I went back to ruminating on that odd scene last night. If that man was indeed a vampire hunter and he'd found the vampire blood bank, what did he want with that actor, Bertram Kensington? Was he trying to get information from him? And what an odd coincidence that Bertram would've been at the vampire blood bank.

I frowned as I thought over Fitz's words last night and glanced up at him. "That actor, last night, the one leaving the blood bank?"

Fitz lifted a brow.

"You said he probably needed money if he was donating blood, right?"

Fitz nodded. "It's my understanding that unlike those who donate blood for charity, most of the human donors at our blood bank are motivated by the payment."

I grinned, clues dropping into place. "The ransom note —I bet he sent it!"

"Come again?"

"Sorry, I forgot to tell you. I saw a ransom note on DI Prescott's desk. It was sent to Petra and was threatening to tell 'him' about her new husband unless she paid up something like £15,000."

Fitz nodded. "Tell who?"

"I think they must've meant Richard, the play's director. Apparently, Richard was super possessive of Petra—that's why she kept her marriage a secret."

"And you think this actor is the one who sent the letter?"

I nodded, feeling more confident the more I thought about it. "I bet he overheard the secret and, being in need of money, saw an opportunity to blackmail Petra and her rich new husband."

Fitz paused his cutting and grinned. "I suspect you're right, Minnie."

I hopped off the wooden stool and grabbed my coat.

Fitz frowned. "Where are you going?

"To the theater! It's a little early, but I bet they'll be there setting up for tonight's performance. If Bertram's that desperate for money, maybe I can pay him to give me information about the vampire hunter and what he wanted from him last night."

Fitz blinked, surprised. "But—with what money?"

I grinned. "I'm not as strapped, thanks to you hiring me." I shrugged. "I won't offer him much, maybe fifty pounds, but maybe he'll take it."

I slid the straps of my huge leather tote back over my shoulder.

"Plus, I have to admit I'm a little intrigued by solving Petra's murder now that I've tagged along for so much of the investigation. I'll ask him about the note and see if he admits to sending it."

Fitz stepped around the workstation, his eyes wide. "Are you mad?" He planted his floury hands on his narrow hips. "If he did send Petra the ransom note and she refused to pay up, maybe he took matters into his own hands and killed her. And now you're going to go down to a dark, empty theater and confront him? Alone?"

I grimaced. "Well... when you put it *that* way..."

He raised his brows. "Take one of the boys with you."

I glanced over my shoulder. "Like Dom?" I shook my head. "I can't ask about the vampire hunter in front of them. Plus, they're working." Not that it was all that busy, but it'd be picking up any minute.

Fitz huffed. "I'd go, but I have to work the kitchen." He sighed and looked off, apparently trying to think up another escort for me. "Gus?"

I shook my head. "He'll still be sleeping for a couple more hours."

Fitz rolled his eyes. "Lazy bones."

I smirked. I didn't know how Fitz did it. He kept both vampire hours and baker's hours. He showed up here first thing every morning to get the bread and pastries baking. He must be one of those people... er... vampires who could function on four hours of sleep a night.

He looked almost pouty. "I hate to suggest it, but... what about the detective?"

I smirked. "Prescott? Like actually get the police involved in official police business?"

He grinned. "Novel thought, I know."

I sighed. "I won't be able to ask about the vampire hunter in front of him..." I brightened. "Actually, why not? I could comment that I'd seen Bertram talking to the same man who'd spoken to Prescott the other night in the lobby of the theater. Maybe it'll startle him into telling me something useful."

Fitz gave me an earnest look. "Be careful, Minnie."

I winked and echoed his words from the previous night. "Always."

18

A BODY

I left Tilda at the tearoom since I had every intention of returning shortly. A light rain tapped against my umbrella as I picked my way across the slick cobblestones to the police station. But when I asked at the front desk for DI Prescott, the officer informed me he was out.

"Do you know when he'll be back?"

"Can't say, miss."

I thanked him and popped back out into the street. The smart thing to do would be to head back to the tearoom and wait for Fitz to close up or see if Dominik or Cho would go with me to the theatre. I glanced to my left and shivered in the cold as I mentally traced the winding path back to the Bath Butler Cafe. I looked down the street ahead of me.

Then again, I was close to the theater. I checked my watch. And it was nearly noon. Surely the cast and crew would be setting up soon for their matinee performance. If I went ahead by myself, it wasn't like I'd be truly alone. There'd be plenty of people around to keep me safe.

That settled it. I strolled toward the theater in the dim

midday sun. Crows cawed overhead, their wings black against the cloudy gray sky as the Bath Abbey bells tolled noon.

A few lights shone in the lobby where a couple of wait-staff in black vests and bow ties set up the bar. I bit my lip. Could I convince them to let me in? I didn't have a ticket, and I was early in any case.

I glanced down the narrow side lane and spotted the big metal garage door partially rolled up. I grinned to myself, feeling clever.

I waited for traffic to clear, then jogged across the street and down the empty lane. I peeked under the garage door, and finding no one looking, closed my umbrella and ducked under. It took a few moments for my eyes to adjust to the dim backstage lighting.

It was even darker than the last time Prescott and I had been back here. Probably because the stage and house lights were off. I listened but heard only a few distant voices and quiet scrapes. Guess I was earlier than I'd thought. I shivered at the eerie emptiness. A rectangle of dim afternoon light shone in under the metal door, calling to me. Maybe I should go back and get one of my friends to come with me—

CLANG!

I startled at the sound of metal falling. What was that? People were clearly here, and this might be my chance to speak with Bertram privately. I steeled myself and crept further inside.

The shadows of ladders, backdrops, mannequins, and ropes loomed all around me, threatening in the dark. I peered around a fake boulder and spotted Ariel, the prop master. A work light shone on a table littered with lace fans, purses, books, needlepoints, and quills. She wore her short, curly brown hair tied back at her neck and again wore those paint-splattered overalls. She pulled a pencil from behind her ear, jotted something down on a notepad, then went back to examining the items. I guessed she was taking inventory or organizing the props for the evening's play.

I slipped past her and crept further back. With only the waitstaff and the prop master around, I was beginning to suspect I'd have some waiting to do before Bertram and the other actors arrived. I rose on my toes and peered further into the backstage area. Even the communal dressing room appeared dark and empty. Creeped out to be back here almost alone, I turned and headed back toward the garage door. I'd return to the tearoom and try again later... this time with a buddy.

As I climbed my way over a coil of rope, an odd-shaped pile up ahead caught my eye. I crept toward it, a witchy wave of unease washing over me. My intuition was ringing alarm bells, the hairs on the back of my neck standing on end. I gulped. At least Ariel was nearby—she'd hear me call out if I needed help. I made a mental note to ask Mim to teach me some self-defense spells.

My heart pounded in my chest as I approached the lumpy shadow on the ground. I pulled my phone out and turned on the flashlight, then held it aloft.

I froze.

There on the ground lay Bertram Kensington, unmoving, his eyes open and vacant. I pressed a trembling hand over my mouth and inched closer. "Bertram?"

He didn't respond. A hammer lay beside his head, and a wound in his hairline shone wet with blood. "Bertram?"

I dropped down beside the man and felt at his neck with trembling fingers. His skin felt cold... no pulse.

I lurched back, stumbling to my feet. The actor was dead!

It took me another moment to find my voice but when I did, I sucked in a deep breath and screamed, "Help!"

19

POLICE WORK

I t didn't take long for DIs Prescott and O'Brien to show up, along with half a dozen uniformed officers. Ariel, who'd heard me screaming and come running, waited with me the whole time. Well, except for the few moments she'd stepped away to mercifully throw on the backstage lights. She'd cracked a few jokes, no doubt trying to make me feel better, but I'd barely heard her. I was too shocked and frightened at having discovered *another* dead body.

Richard, Elinor, Harvey, and the rest of the actors all filtered in soon after. They'd been scheduled to show up for their first performance of the afternoon and instead had walked into another crime scene.

As police officers with evidence bags and various kits combed backstage, Prescott and O'Brien stood with their backs to the stage and sat the rest of us in the front rows of the theatre. Ariel, Richard, Elinor, Harvey, and I sat before them. Elinor crossed her arms and legs, grumbling about what an inconvenience this all was.

O'Brien shot her a hard look. "Ma'am. This is more than an inconvenience. It's a murder investigation."

Richard lifted a finger on his bandaged hand. "Horrible tragedy, truly. But... why have you pulled *our* group aside?" He raised a thick brow at me. "*Most* of us weren't even here when it happened."

Prescott's gaze lingered on me before he addressed the director. "Where were you, exactly, this afternoon?"

Richard stroked his beard. "Why, in my flat. Napping before the evening's work."

As Prescott jotted down notes in his phone, O'Brien narrowed his eyes at the director. "Can anyone corroborate this?"

Richard scoffed. "I—I was alone. So... no, I suppose not. But I didn't kill that man, if that's what you're getting at."

O'Brien repeated the question to Harvey and Elinor. Both claimed they were similarly alone in their own homes, Harvey eating a light meal and Elinor going through her vocal warm-ups.

Ariel lifted a palm. "I came down here early, about an hour ago. I wanted to get a jump on organizing the props."

Richard shot her a curious look.

O'Brien leaned back against the tall stage and crossed his ankles. "And did you see anyone else while you were here?"

Ariel lifted her eyes to the sparkling chandelier over-head. "Uh... I guess I saw Roy and Dirk. They're a couple of stagehands."

Prescott tapped away at his phone, taking notes.

O'Brien nodded for her to continue, but she just shrugged. "I don't know. That's all I remember."

Prescott shot me a puzzled look. "And you, Minnie? What were you doing here?"

Good question. The others all swiveled to stare, and my cheeks grew hot under their gazes. What to say?

I couldn't admit that I wanted to ask Bertram about the vampire hunter who'd apprehended him outside the blood bank.

And I wasn't ready to air my suspicions that Bertram had blackmailed Petra over her secret marriage. His murder had to be connected to Petra's. I mean, what were the odds that two actors in the same production would be murdered in the same theater within days of each other? Regardless, though, I wasn't a detective. If I pretended I wanted to interrogate Bertram about the blackmail, Prescott would rightfully think that I was majorly overstepping my bounds. Plus, the much less sympathetic O'Brien would probably arrest me for interfering in an ongoing murder investigation.

"Minnie?"

I gulped as I realized Prescott had been waiting a long time for my answer.

Ariel reached over and squeezed my forearm. "I offered to give Minnie a backstage tour."

Prescott frowned. "You two know each other?"

I shot Ariel a puzzled look but decided to go with it. I guessed we *were* witchy sisters, after all. I plastered on a weak smile. "We're new friends."

Elinor snorted. "Oh, I'm sure you were going to give her a *very* thorough tour, weren't you?"

Ariel's face turned bright red, and she snatched her hand back from my arm.

Elinor continued, a cruel curl to her lip. "*Close* friends, are you?"

Ariel dropped her gaze to her lap.

I frowned at the brunette actress. I wasn't sure exactly what she was implying, but she was acting like a bully.

O'Brien's sharp gaze missed none of it. He grunted. "Okay, then."

While I understood the detectives being suspicious of this group—including me—I couldn't help the sneaking feeling that the killer wasn't among us. Maybe I should share at least part of my theory.

I tentatively raised my hand. "Prescott. Could I have a word?" I gulped. "In private?"

He looked surprised but nodded. We walked up the aisle toward the front of the house together, away from the others.

"Minnie, what's going on?"

I raised my brows and shot him an earnest look. "I think it might've been Petra's husband."

He looked doubtful. "Mr. Rossi?"

I nodded. "I'm pretty sure Bertram sent that letter blackmailing Petra."

He frowned. "How do you know about that?"

I winced. "Saw it on your desk, sorry. But Bertram needed money."

Prescott frowned deeper. "Again, how do you know about that?"

"Uh..." I fished around for a plausible explanation that didn't involve vampires and blood. I opened my mouth to mention seeing Bertram talking to trenchcoat guy, but realized that if Prescott asked the alleged vampire hunter about it, it might link me (and worse, Fitz and Gus) to the vampire blood bank. "Uh...just kind of a feeling, you know? He really wanted some free drinks the other night, remember?"

He looked unconvinced. "Okay..."

I splayed my hands. "Let's say Petra's husband regretted marrying her. He's rich, right? And Harvey mentioned that he and Petra had been fighting because he wanted her to sign a prenup *after* the fact. She refuses, they're already having regrets, and he's afraid she'll take half of his money if they get divorced, so he kills her." I raised my brows. "He admitted to being at the theater the night she died, and unlike Harvey and Richard, he doesn't have an alibi, right?"

Prescott shifted on his feet and blew out a heavy breath. "Okay... but I have a hard time believing these two deaths are unrelated. So if Mr. Rossi killed his wife, why then kill Bertram?"

I shrugged. "Maybe Bertram witnessed it? He could've tried to blackmail Mr. Rossi for even more money." I winced. "Honestly, I'm not sure about that part."

Prescott pressed his lips together and flashed his eyes at me. "I appreciate the effort, but I've got this, Minnie." His throat bobbed. "I'll talk to O'Brien. I know you found the body, but I'm sure you didn't have anything to do with this. You're free to go. And don't lurk around dark buildings anymore."

I gave him a weak grin.

He frowned. "And look, I hope this doesn't sound too harsh, but... you're not a detective. This case is dangerous business, and frankly out of your league. I know you're maybe just trying to impress me or get my attention but... this isn't the way to do it."

Come again?

"I'm sorry if this is hard to hear, but I need you to hear it. I meant what I said last night. It's nothing to do with you, but I just don't have time for a love life right now. I'm sorry."

He pressed his lips together, then turned and walked back toward O'Brien and the others.

I stared after him for a moment, shocked. I was partly relieved that he hadn't picked up on the fact that I'd been snooping around for reasons related to my vampire friends. At the same time, that rebuke stung!

I turned and walked toward the lobby, my heart heavy.

Maybe he was right. The case wasn't my business, and I did need to be more careful—that could've been me, who took a hammer to the head!

I frowned as I climbed past the rows of seats. Then again, I did find Bertram's body—and was there for the discovery of Petra's, as well. And, I had solved a couple of murders already. It wasn't like I was a *complete* newbie at it. Was it so crazy to think I might be able to help solve another one?

Plus, my witchy hunches were useful, and I had a gut feeling that I was onto something. These murders had something to do with Petra's secret marriage—I could feel it. I set my jaw. I had an interest in this case, and I was going to get to the bottom of it—with or without Prescott's approval.

20

THE FUNERAL

The next morning, I pulled out my laptop and lounged in bed with Tilda. A light rain tapped at my attic window, the sky gray and my four-poster feeling cozier than ever. Fueled by both a desire to get justice for Petra and Bertram and annoyance with DI Prescott, I searched online for information about Petra. Almost immediately, I found a notice for her funeral, which was being held in an hour at Bath Abbey.

I glanced toward the rain-spattered window with a lack of enthusiasm. From the window seat, I could easily spot the Gothic tower of the church and the Roman baths right beside it. So it wasn't like it was a far walk, but I was loath to get out of my warm bed with my purring familiar. Then again, how else was I going to gather information to prove my current theory that Petra's secret husband, Mr. Rossi, had killed both her and the actor whose body I'd discovered?

I heaved a great sigh and threw back the sheets and quilt. Tilda lifted her head, blinked her bright eyes, and then tucked her nose back under her tail.

I shot her a wistful look. "I don't blame you."

I opened the ancient wood wardrobe and pulled out my black dress and then my black wool stockings and made myself presentable. I wound my long dark hair into a bun at the nape of my neck and grabbed my wedge ankle booties, then crept downstairs. I had time to eat a quick breakfast of toast and a banana, quietly so as not to wake my vampire friend, then walked the drizzly streets of Bath the short distance to the abbey.

I took a program from the usher at the door and couldn't help but draw a parallel to taking a program at the door for the play. This wasn't a dramatization, but a real-life tragedy, though. I filed inside behind an older couple and was struck with awe at the huge proportions inside. The carved ceiling and strong pillars shone a brilliant white, lit by flickering candles and the enormous stained glass window behind the pulpit.

The seemingly endless rows of pews stood mostly empty. I'd been to one funeral here previously for a well-connected member of the aristocracy, and the place had been packed with hundreds of mourners. Petra's was a more intimate affair, which meant my presence would be more noticeable.

I squared my shoulders and reminded myself I didn't need to feel awkward about being here. I'd seen her last performance and been among the group who discovered her body—I had a right to pay my respects. I was also determined to catch her killer.

I filed down the center aisle toward the front of the church and the thirty or so mourners who took up the first several rows of pews. I scanned the crowd and spotted a few familiar faces. Mr. Rossi, Petra's secret husband, sat up front beside an older couple and some others I assumed were family. In the second row, Harvey sat beside Ariel and a few others who seemed vaguely familiar—other members of the cast and crew, I assumed. Richard sat across the aisle from them—down the same row as DIs Prescott and O'Brien.

My stomach clenched as Prescott's gaze skimmed over me. He did a double take, then gaped. I wiggled my fingers in a brief wave, then slid down the pew to my left, about as far away as I could get from him. Once I sat, I kept my gaze studiously straight ahead for a few minutes, not daring to look in Prescott's direction. He probably assumed I was stalking him at this point, but I wasn't here for him, and I wasn't about to make him think I was by looking his way.

Eventually, I tested the waters and checked the other side of the aisle. Petra's rival, Elinor, sat near Richard. Interesting that she was attending this morning, considering she and Petra had been at odds. Maybe it was just for face value, since the rest of the cast and crew seemed to be here to pay their respects.

The preacher began his sermon shortly after, with Petra's urn situated among beautiful bouquets of flowers behind him. Petra's sister and father spoke tearfully about what a lively, creative young woman she'd always been, and a short while later the service concluded.

Mr. Rossi stood with Petra's family in a receiving line near the urn, and I joined the queue to give them my condolences. A little commotion up ahead caused the rest of the quiet murmur of conversation to go silent.

"Mother! Hold your tongue!" Mr. Rossi, his red face stained with tears, scowled at a tiny woman with dark, curly hair.

She wore an elegant gown, her neck and wrists bejeweled with glittering gems. She lifted her sharp nose in the air. "It's true! I know you miss her, but she was not here for love. She wanted our money!" Her Italian accent was even heavier than her son's.

"Come now, this is highly inappropriate." Petra's father, a man with a white mustache and matching hair, stepped toward the woman who was evidently Mr. Rossi's mother.

She turned to him. "No offense intended, sir, but what did your daughter and my son have in common, huh? She was a miner."

The father frowned. "A what?"

"She was panning for jewels? How you say?"

Elinor, who stood just ahead of me in line, lifted her chin and called out, "A gold digger?"

The little Italian lady pointed at her. "Thank you. Yes, she was a gold digger."

Richard turned and shot Elinor a flat look, but she smirked, clearly proud of herself. She was moving up my list of suspects.

Petra's sister huffed. "This is unbelievable! How dare you!"

Mr. Rossi jumped in-between his mother and sister-in-law, arms outstretched to keep them apart. "Stop this!" He spun to face his mother. "It's too much! You're the one who convinced me to ask Petra for a prenup after we were already married!"

His mother nodded. "Yes. It's smart."

He sniffled. "No, Mother! It made us fight! We spent the last week of our lives together fighting. I'll always regret it." He dissolved into sobs, and his mother wrapped him in a hug, patting his back.

I tried not to look too shocked, but wow. Quite a scene. I frowned, suddenly feeling less certain of my theory that Mr. Rossi was our killer. He seemed to have genuine feelings for Petra, and at least now I knew what it was they'd been fighting about. It seemed his mother had pressured him into asking for the prenup to protect the family money, and no wonder it'd led to some strife between him and his new wife. But it didn't seem like Mr. Rossi himself was the one who cared about the money, and I suddenly doubted that he'd had the motive to kill Petra or Bertram.

After a few moments, Mr. Rossi rejoined the receiving line, still sniffling, and we began to move forward again. As I waited behind Elinor, my mind raced to put the puzzle together. The top suspects seemed to be Richard—so possessive of Petra. And yet, he had an airtight alibi. Harvey had been Petra's best friend, and though they'd argued, he seemed to genuinely care about and want the best for her. Plus, he also had an alibi and didn't obviously gain anything from her death.

I bit my lip and shuffled forward. Ariel seemed to be keeping something from me; I wasn't sure what, though. She had the opportunity to kill Petra and Bertram—in fact, I'd seen her at the theatre right before I'd discovered his body yesterday. She'd told me herself that she and Petra used to be close—maybe they'd had a falling out and she'd finally decided to enact some revenge? Still, it didn't seem like she'd benefit much from killing her or Bertram. Plus, maybe it was just our shared witchy connection, but I kind of liked and trusted Ariel. In fact, she'd covered for me yesterday. I wanted to thank her... and ask her why she'd done it.

Which left Mr. Rossi, who was quickly seeming less guilty in my mind, and Elinor. The rival actress was far from upset over Petra's death and had finally gotten her long-coveted starring role. She clearly enjoyed being in the spot-light, and in that short time between disappearing from the meet the cast party and Petra's body being discovered, she might've had time to kill her. As I stared at her back, mulling it over, I made a startling discovery.

Gray fur stuck to the back of her black cardigan. Lots of it. My jaw dropped. According to Harvey, someone had covered the inside of Petra's costume with cat hair the night she was killed. It seemed like just the kind of mean-spirited trick Elinor might pull.

I reached forward and plucked up a clump of it.

Elinor spun at my touch and scowled at me. "Excuse you!"

I held up the hair and raised my brows. "Do you own a cat?"

She frowned and then rolled her eyes. "Yes. The hair gets everywhere. Get over it."

She turned back to face forward, but I tapped her shoulder, and she turned to face me again.

"What?!"

I lowered my voice to a whisper. "You're the one who put cat hair in Petra's costume, aren't you?"

Her mouth fell open, then her lips curled into a sneer. "I don't know what you're talking about."

I glared at her. "I'll give the hairs to that detective I know. All they have to do is DNA test it against the ones found in Petra's costume, and once it's a match, they'll know you did it."

Her sneer faded into a scowl, and she pursed her lips tight together. "They can't do that."

I shot her a challenging look back. Truly, I wasn't sure if they could, but I hoped she wouldn't call my bluff.

We glared at each other for a few more moments, then she huffed and hissed back, "Fine! I planted the hair in her costume. So what?"

I shook my head at her. "You triggered her allergies so

she'd have to take medicine. Medicine you *knew* made her groggy." I raised my brows. "So she wouldn't be able to fight back when you killed her."

Elinor paled and glanced around, her eyes wide. She leaned forward and bared her teeth. "Keep your voice down. I did it just to ruin her performance. I knew she'd get all sneezy and then drowsy, sure—but that's it." She rolled her eyes. "I just wanted to make her look bad. She was the golden girl, Richard's perfect little muse, couldn't do anything wrong." She shook her head. "I was so tired of working so hard and being practically invisible!" She looked me up and down. "But I did *not* kill her!"

We shuffled forward, and Elinor spun to face Petra's father. She took his hand and rearranged her features into an expression of pained sympathy. "I'm so sorry for your loss. Your daughter and I acted together. She'll be truly missed."

I raised my brows. *Wow*. She was a good actress... which meant she could easily have been lying just now about not killing Petra.

Richard, just ahead of Elinor in line, shook hands with Petra's older sister. She looked a lot like the actress. Richard used his non-bandaged hand to reach behind her ear and pull his flower trick. He produced a lily.

"A flower for a beautiful flower."

The sister frowned, then glanced behind her. "Did you take this from one of the flower arrangements?"

Richard gave an awkward chuckle and moved on to Mr. Rossi. I scoffed. Wow—he used that move on everyone, and it was almost never appropriate.

I murmured my condolences to Petra's father next, though my mind was elsewhere, mulling over the details of the case. At least I'd solved the mystery of who'd triggered

Petra's allergies. But could the killer really have been someone other than Elinor?

Maybe the murderer saw Petra being drugged and defenseless as their time to strike. Prescott told me the knife used to kill her had been swiped from the lobby bar, which suggested a crime of opportunity more than one that'd been planned out. But who was the culprit?

21

WITCHY SISTERS

After I made my way down the receiving line, I headed toward the exit. The wake after was just for friends and family. Plus, I had a lot of work to do for the tearoom.

"Minnie?"

I knew that voice. I winced and turned to my left. DI Prescott sat alone in a pew, his phone in his hand (no doubt taking more notes). He looked handsome in a black suit, and for a moment I was tempted to smile and flirt, like we had before our awkward date. Then I remembered he likely wanted to stake some of my best friends, and I grew serious.

"Prescott."

He cleared his throat and rose, then walked toward me. "I, uh—I didn't expect to see you here this morning."

I shrugged. "I wanted to pay my respects."

He lifted a dark brow. "I didn't realize you and Petra were close." He darted a glance toward the double doors of the church, where Ariel stood chatting with Harvey. "Then again, I didn't realize you and the prop master were friendly, either."

Sounded like Prescott was fishing for information. Well, if he wasn't going to level with me about the guy in the trench coat, I didn't think I needed to elaborate, either. I lifted my nose. "There's a lot you don't know about me. See you around."

I spun on my heel before he could respond and strode toward the exit, grinning. I didn't want him to even remotely get the idea that I'd shown up today hoping to see him. Plus, let him think I was a little mysterious.

As I neared Ariel and Harvey, the prop master glanced my way. "Oh, Minnie. I was, uh, hoping to have a word?"

Harvey dabbed his eyes with a tissue. "I'll see you later at rehearsal." He patted Ariel's shoulder, then moved off to join another group of people from the production.

She wrapped her black shawl around her and edged closer. "Think we could chat?"

I nodded. "I was hoping to speak with you, too." I grinned. "I owe you one for yesterday."

She shrugged.

"Can I buy you a coffee?"

"Deal."

We walked outside and down the steps into the square. Ariel led the way to her favorite spot, tucked down a nearby narrow lane. The shop was hip, clean, and sparsely decorated aside from a little jungle of potted plants and few kids typing away at laptops—students, I guessed. We ordered our drinks—a mocha for me and coffee, black for her. After they were made, we settled at a table in a quiet corner.

I wrapped my chilly hands around my steaming mug. "Thanks again. For covering for me yesterday." I bit my lip. "Why did you, by the way?"

Ariel leaned back in her chair and nodded, her lips pressed tight together. Today she'd ditched the paint-splattered overalls for a black turtleneck under a black corduroy jumper dress. She'd piled her curly hair into a bun on top of her head, a few tendrils framing her face.

"That's what I wanted to talk about, too. I guess I felt a sort of witchy sister loyalty, and I could tell you were floundering." She gave me a weak grin.

I let out a dry chuckle. "I was."

She nodded. "Witches got to stick together."

I chuckled. "Speaking of, want me to hex Elinor?" I shook my head. "She was being such a bully to you."

She shrugged. "What's new."

I sniffed. "Not that I could hex her anyway. I'm not the best at magic."

"Thanks, anyway." She leaned forward, her gaze intense. "Magic sisterhood aside, I wanted to talk to you to make sure I wasn't being a dummy. I'm not about to go lying for the person who murdered Petra and Bertram." She raised her brows. "So what were you *really* doing at the theater yesterday afternoon?"

"Fair question." I nodded, thinking over my options. I could lie, but I doubted I'd be able to think up a very good one. And in any case, despite the evidence stacked against her, my gut told me to trust Ariel. Maybe it came from that same sense of foolish loyalty that had prompted her to cover for me, but I wanted to be honest with her.

"I can't tell you all the details, but I thought Bertram might be connected with someone who I believe is hunting some friends of mine. I want to find him to have a word."

She frowned and leaned forward, lowering her voice. "There's a witch hunter in town?"

I winced. "No. I'm sorry, I can't really go into it any more."

She bit her lip, then took a sip of her coffee.

I scooted forward, wanting her to believe me. "I promise you I didn't kill Petra or Bertram or anyone! The other reason I wanted to speak to Bertram was because I suspect he was blackmailing Petra."

Ariel lowered her mug. "Go on."

I licked my lips. "Someone sent Petra a note, threatening to tell 'him' about her secret marriage unless she paid up. Bertram seemed desperate for money, and I think he was threatening to tell Richard."

Ariel nodded. "Listen, maybe it's the whole witch thing, but I trust you." Her throat bobbed. "Petra and I dated, years ago. I was heartbroken when she called it off... not sure I ever got over her, to tell you the truth." She sniffed. "She was rude to me most of the time, barely acknowledged I existed after, but a couple of days ago, she apologized out of nowhere. She told me about her secret marriage, that she was quitting acting, and that she was sorry for how things had ended between us."

I blinked. "Wow."

Ariel nodded. "Yeah. I was stunned... and then crushed that she'd gotten married." She sighed. "You'd think I'd be over it by now."

I shot her a sympathetic look. "Hearts can take a long time to heal." While I didn't have any desire to get back with Desmond, I still felt my fair share of anger, hurt, and resentment toward him.

Ariel groaned and hung her head. "It was stupid of me, but a bunch of us went out after work one night. I was tipsy and sad and... I told a few people about it all." She glanced up at me, her brow pinched with pain. "What if that's what got her killed? I'm sure that's how Bertram, or whoever blackmailed Petra, learned about her secret marriage. It was my fault."

I winced. "Oh, don't think like that. You don't know for sure—Petra told Harvey too, and a few others. He might've heard some other way. And even if he did hear from you, it was his decision to blackmail her and get involved in some shady dealings." I shook my head. "None of this is your fault."

She wiped some tears from her eyes and shot me a sad smile. "Thanks."

I took another sip of my chocolatey drink, then took a deep breath. "Can I ask you about what you told me the night of the Equinox? What did you mean about Richard being possessive? Do you still think he killed Petra?"

She shook her head, groaning. "I don't know anymore. This week has been... exhausting." She let out a heavy sigh. "But, yeah, I think it's possible he's the killer."

"He has an alibi, though. I was with him in the lobby and when he discovered Petra's body."

Ariel nodded. "I know. But you should've seen the way he treated her. He got furious anytime she talked to other men aside from running her lines. He'd yell at her or give her the silent treatment."

I grunted. "Sounds like that'd make life really difficult for Petra."

A mischievous smile tugged at the corner of her lips as she gazed down into her coffee. "It did, except Richard never suspected she might be getting around all that by being with a lady." She chuckled. "We flew under the radar, so to speak, when we were together."

I frowned. "That's terrible, though. Why'd she put up with it for so long?"

Ariel gave me a flat look. "She didn't have much choice, not if she wanted to succeed in her career. Richard is powerful and well-connected in the UK theater community. He has the power to make or break your career." She shook her head. "Some men get like that. He thought he owned her or something." She lifted her hand dramatically. "She was his star!" Her shoulders slumped. "I don't blame her for wanting to retire and escape it all. I kind of envy her, really."

I pressed my lips together. What a terrible working environment. Ariel made Richard sound like a tyrant.

"Oh—one more thing."

Ariel looked up.

"I wanted to ask you about Petra's cat allergies. Elinor just admitted to planting cat hair in her costume that night."

Ariel scoffed. "That shrew! I knew it was her." She shook her head. "Petra had terrible cat allergies. She was really suffering that night."

"Did you give her some antihistamines?"

Ariel nodded. "Harvey did, too. I think she took at least three or four to get through the performance. I was surprised she could keep her eyes open."

We finished our drinks, chatted a bit more about the Equinox celebration, and then parted ways. I headed home to grab my laptop and then planned to work from the tearoom. I hoped I'd been right to trust Ariel with all I'd told her.

My stomach twisted. I'd thought Desmond was my forever person, and look how wrong I'd been there! What if Ariel was crushed when Petra told her she'd been married and couldn't stand to see her with anyone else? Maybe she killed Petra out of hurt and anger—I could definitely relate to having those feelings toward an ex, though I wasn't murderous over them. Maybe Bertram witnessed it and knew too much, so she killed him too.

My brain hurt from trying to sort all the information out. Hopefully, some time spent with Fitz in the tearoom's cozy kitchen—and maybe a scone or two—would help clear it up.

22

ACCUSATION

I dashed into the tearoom through the alley door with my bag and Tilda huddled under my jacket. The light drizzle had turned into a heavy rain about halfway through my walk, and my hair was soaked.

Fitz spun around as I shut the door behind me. "Afternoon."

I grinned. "Hi." I waved him off before he could say anything. "I know, I know. I'm taking Tilda straight through to the dining room."

He raised a brow at my black cat. "Afternoon, Tilda."

She meowed back as we hurried past his workstation. I used my foot to push the swinging door open and set Tilda down. She raised her tail high and immediately jogged over to Leo, who was taking an order.

I hefted my laptop back up, then lay it on the stool. As I shrugged out of my wet jacket, Fitz came around the side of the workstation. "It's really coming down out there, isn't it?"

I chuckled and threw my coat on the stool on top of my bag. "And of course, I forgot my umbrella."

"Here."

I blinked in surprise as Fitz pulled the kitchen towel from his waist apron and gently wiped my hairline dry. I froze as he dried the other side of my forehead, then my cheeks. He shot me a small grin, then handed me the towel and returned to his usual spot.

My heart hammered in my chest, and my cheeks burned hot. If I'd been missing the butterflies with Prescott, I now knew where to find them. I gulped and found my breath again. Fitz had stood so close, dried my face so gently. I mentally shook myself—I'd be replaying that moment in my head later and analyzing every little look and touch.

In the meantime, I needed to act like a normal human. I cleared my throat and pulled out the other stool. "Thanks." I shot him an awkward smile, my cheeks still hot, and held up the towel.

He nodded, grinning.

I frowned down at the table. Flour dusted the butcher block surface and Fitz went back to rolling dough. "What're you making?"

He set down the rolling pin and held up an oval cookie cutter. "Sugar cookies. I had some requests for Easter shapes."

I grinned. "That's fun. A little early though."

He nodded. "Just wanted to practice. I haven't made them in quite some time." He glanced up. "Would you want to help me decorate the next batch?" He tipped his head toward the cooling racks on the counters. One rack held plain baked cookies, while the other rack was already decorated in pastel pinks, purples, and blues.

"How fun." I grinned. "I'd love to."

"Good." He shook his head and held up his hands. "Be prepared, though. The food dye in the frosting stains."

His big hands were tie-dyed in spring colors, especially around the edges of his fingernails.

I grinned. "I'll consider myself warned." As I stared at those strong hands, a piece of the puzzle slid into place.

"Minnie? Is everything alright?"

I blinked at him, my mind a million miles away. "Fitz, that's it!" I leapt off the stool and grabbed my coat, sliding my arm back into the sleeve. All the random pieces of the murder mysteries began sliding into place. "The food dye! That's it!"

I shrugged on my jacket and grabbed my bag. "Thank you!" I planted my hands on Fitz's shoulder, rose on my toes, giddy, and gave him a quick kiss on the cheek.

He sucked in a quick breath and stared wide-eyed at me, his pale cheeks turning pink. I'd made a vampire blush!

I grinned and ran for the back door.

"Where are you going?"

I grinned and waved. "To solve the murders! I'll be back soon."

I dashed back out into the alley, the metal door clanging shut behind me. I grabbed my phone and called DI Prescott. When he didn't pick up, I tried his partner, DI O'Brien. I'd saved their numbers from earlier cases. I got his voicemail too, so as I sped through the streets, I tried the station.

"I'm sorry, but both detectives are currently away from their desks."

I stopped on a street corner. "Can you tell me where I can find them?"

"Uh... hold on a moment."

I jiggled my leg impatiently.

"They're working a case down at the Bath Theatre Royal."

Perfect! "Thank you!" I took a hard left and dashed

toward the theater, replaying all the evidence in my mind.
That little glimpse of the frosting stains on Fitz's hand had
linked all the seemingly disconnected clues together—the
secret marriage, Petra's plan to retire, Richard's possessive-
ness, the blood packet in the bin, the cat hair, the backstage
tour, the bandaged hand!

It all made sense. I just hoped Prescott had the sense to
listen to me and wouldn't dismiss me outright because he
thought I was, as he'd put it, "out of my league."

It only took me minutes to reach the theater. I found the
doors to the lobby unlocked. I yanked them open and strode
through.

The gal behind the bar raised her arm. "Hey! Wait! You
can't—"

I ignored her and threw open the doors to the theater,
striding down the center aisle. A little commotion on stage
immediately drew my eye.

Prescott and O'Brien stood beside several uniformed
officers, two of them handcuffing Ariel. Richard, Harvey,
Elinor, and a dozen other cast and crew stood nearby,
gawking.

One of the officers read Ariel her rights. "You have the
right to remain—"

"Wait!"

They all looked up at me. I jogged down the red center
carpet, gulping to catch my breath. I'd practically run the
whole way from the tearoom. I dragged my sleeve across my
forehead, pulling my soaking wet hair back.

"Wait!" I huffed, trying to breathe. "She's—innocent!"

Ariel shot me a grateful look.

O'Brien looked like he wanted to kill me, and Prescott's
cheeks burned a deep purple.

The older detective crossed his arms from on stage and

glared down at me. He stepped his feet wider. "Is that so? What evidence do you have to—"

I pointed at Richard. "It was him. It was Richard, the director." I tossed my leather bag onto the nearest theater seat and sucked in a breath.

23

ARREST

E linor, who stood beside him, recoiled, and Harvey
gasped.

Ariel nodded, her hands still cuffed behind her
back. "I knew it!"

O'Brien's dark, beady eyes blazed. "Just because you're
the girlfriend of an officer, it doesn't make you—"

"I'm not his girlfriend!" I blurted at the same time
Prescott insisted, "She's *not* my girlfriend."

We frowned at each other. Did he have to sound so
indignant about it?

I planted my hands on the stage and tried to hoist myself
up, only to find it was way too tall and I didn't have the
upper body strength. With as much dignity as I could
muster, I dropped back down and walked around the side,
taking the stairs up.

I looked between Prescott and O'Brien. "I know I'm not
an officer of the law, but hear me out." I raised my brows at
Prescott. "Please."

When neither spoke, I took that as a "yes."

I pointed at Elinor. "Elinor planted cat hair inside Petra's costume the night she died to ruin her performance. She wanted to trigger a reaction, causing Petra to sneeze and cough and ultimately to get groggy from taking antihistamines."

Elinor shrugged. "Okay, but I didn't kill her."

I shook my head. "No, you didn't. But you set the stage for Richard to." I mentally gave myself props for the unintentional pun, then continued. "The late Bertram Kensington overheard Ariel talking about Petra's secret marriage or heard it somehow through the grapevine. He tried to blackmail her and her new husband for money. When she ignored his threats, I suspect Bertram went to Richard, offering information for money."

Richard scoffed. "This is preposterous. Again, I have an alibi. Witnesses were with me from the time the curtain fell to the time I discovered Petra's body—in front of a group!"

I nodded. "I'll explain that bit. When Richard learned of the secret marriage, he was furious. Multiple people have testified that he was insanely possessive and jealous of Petra and wouldn't let other men near her. She was *his* muse. When he learned she'd not only married, but was planning to retire, he was possessed by a murderous rage."

Maybe it was being on stage, but I suddenly found myself being quite dramatic.

"But what could he do? Probably that very night, he saw an opportunity to get his revenge. With Petra groggy from the allergy medicine, he knew she'd be defenseless—unconscious, no doubt. But how to kill her?"

I turned to Richard. He glared at me, his lip curled. "I think he got the idea partway through the play. While backstage, he stole a blood packet from props, and then at the party after, stole the knife from the lobby bar and tucked both up his sleeve."

Ariel raised her brow at the director. "You stole the blood packet?"

He scoffed. "Nonsense. Why would I?"

"Because you planned to use your skills as a former magician to do a trick. You waited a bit, till you suspected Petra had passed out. When Harvey suggested someone should check on her, you offered a backstage tour—so you'd have witnesses."

Richard's face turned a deep purple. I was on the right track.

I turned to the detectives. "When Richard sat beside Petra on the couch, she was alive—sleeping deeply from the antihistamines—but alive."

Harvey covered his mouth. "No." He shook his head. "I was there too. The blood!"

I nodded. "It's all about the blood, actually. Richard reached a hand behind Petra's back, opened the blood packet with sleight of hand, and then held his bloody palm up for everyone to see."

Harvey frowned. "And then I fainted?"

I nodded. "And everyone else, including me, ran out to get help. Richard shouted that she was dead, and so we assumed from all the 'blood' that she was."

I glared at the director. "But she wasn't—not yet. You stabbed her then with the knife. She was defenseless, and you killed her because if you couldn't have her all to your-self, no one could."

"You coward!" Ariel hissed.

Elinor backed away from Richard.

He scoffed and held up his hands, one bandaged. "Where's your proof? This is all conjecture. Why are we even listening to this random girl?!"

DI O'Brien raised a bushy brow at me. "It's an interesting theory. But as he says... do you have proof?"

I gulped. "I think so." I pointed at Richard's left hand. "The day after Petra died, Richard sported those bandages. He claimed he'd burned his hand, but I think if they're removed, you'll find that he covered it up because his skin is stained from the fake blood."

Ariel gasped. "It's true! That stuff is crazy hard to get off. It stains your skin for days."

I grinned. Just like the dye from the frosting on Fitz's hands.

O'Brien turned to Richard. "All right, let's see."

The director backed up, shaking his head. "My hand's burned! You're not a doctor! I don't have to show you!"

O'Brien nodded to a uniformed officer, who advanced on the director. "Sir. Please remove your bandages."

Trembling, his jaw set, Richard unwound the gauze from his hand and held it up so we all could see. It was pinkish, with red dye stuck in the lines and creases—but no burn.

Prescott's mouth fell open. He blinked at me, wide-eyed, then turned back to Richard. "Care to explain that?"

Richard's throat bobbed. "I, uh—the burn must've healed quickly."

Prescott frowned. "I meant the fact that your hand is stained."

"It's... nothing!"

Harvey pointed at him. "You killed Bertram, too! Why?"

The director snapped, his face bright red, a vein bulging in his neck. "Because he saw me stabbing her in her dressing room and the creep tried to blackmail me to keep quiet about it!" Spit flew from his mouth, illuminated by the bright stage lights.

Elinor gasped.

The director bared his teeth and shouted at all of us. "She was mine! She owed me everything! How dare she think she could just leave!"

Ariel and I exchanged shocked looks, and O'Brien tipped his head toward the officers. "Arrest him."

Richard stumbled backward toward the curtain, eyeing the wings as though he was about to make a break for it, but Harvey darted forward, cutting off his escape route. "You killed Petra. You're a monster."

The officers released Ariel and instead cuffed Richard as they read him his rights.

The prop master, back in her usual overalls, marched up to Richard and slapped him. "You're awful! And to think you were going to let me take the fall for you. Despicable!"

She lifted her nose in the air and strolled over to me. "That was impressive."

I grinned. "Thanks. You too."

She smirked, though the humor quickly faded. "Thank you. If it wasn't for you, I'd be behind bars."

I shook my head. "I'm sorry. Are you okay? That must've been pretty tough to hear."

She glared at Richard as the police finished reading him his rights and marched him offstage. "He's a pig, and I hope he rots behind bars." She huffed and turned to me. "Thanks for getting justice for Petra. It would've eaten away at me if I never knew what happened to her." She sucked in a breath and straightened. "I actually think this will give me some closure. I've been so hung up on Petra for years now." She hung her head. "It's probably time I got back out there and moved on with my life."

Prescott slowly approached, and Ariel raised her brows at me. "Maybe I'll see you at the pub for the Solstice."

I grinned. "Sounds great." I had another witch friend!

Prescott winced. "Hey. Nice job."

I grinned. "Even for someone who was way out of their league?"

"Yeah." He dropped his head and rubbed the back of his neck. "I'm sorry about that. I hope you know I just didn't want you to get hurt."

I nodded. "I know. You have to admit, I'm not a bad amateur detective, though."

He gave me a small grin, the bags still heavy under his eyes. "Okay. I admit it. But please consider retiring? Bath is a more dangerous place than it looks. There are things you couldn't even imagine lurking just around the corner." He looked haunted as he said it.

My stomach sank. There it was again—that reminder that he probably viewed witches and vampires as nothing but menacing fiends.

He sucked in a breath over his teeth. "We okay?"

I nodded. "Sure."

I hoped so.

24

CLOSURE

The very next day, I received a life-changing letter —my divorce had gone through! When I told the guys at the tearoom the good news, they insisted we go out for drinks that night to celebrate, both the divorce being finalized and my part in helping solve a double murder. I invited Fitz along, of course, and Gus too, as soon as he woke up later that afternoon.

Our whole party squeezed into the long corner table in the Heart of the Hart pub, just around the corner. A crackling fire blazed in the big fireplace, and the cozy place hummed with conversation and laughter. Apparently the guys were regulars here, so the waitress only lifted a brow, but didn't say anything when Leo carried Tilda in. She now sat in his lap across from me, gingerly sniffing at his roast chicken salad.

He held up a piece of chicken to me. "Can I give her some?"

She whipped her head to look at me, her yellow eyes wide. Meow! "Say yes!"

I froze, then shook myself. I could've sworn Tilda just

spoke...but glancing around the table, no one else seemed to have noticed.

Leo raised his brows. "Minnie?"

I shrugged it off and nodded. "You spoiled cat."

She gobbled up the offered treat, then nuzzled Leo's hand, blatantly begging for more. I shook my head at her. She had the macho man wrapped around her little claw. And could she talk or was that just my imagination? I probably just needed to get a good night's sleep.

Aldric sat at the head of the table, eyes closed, savoring every bite of his double fudge brownie, while Dominik and Cho argued over dating advice for Calvin.

"You took her to a play?" Cho shook his head. "Now she's going to expect flowers, jewelry, to be wined and dined every time." He leaned across the table. "Trust me. You've got to walk it back. Keep it casual."

Calvin frowned. "What do you mean?"

Dominik finished a sip of his whiskey and reached a hand out. "Don't listen to this guy. You just be yourself. That's why she's going out with you. If you want to treat her, do it."

Calvin, his brows pinched with confusion, looked between the two men, while Aldric just chuckled his deep rumbling laugh and ate his dessert for dinner.

Cho rounded on Dom. "But where does it stop? He'll just have to keep escalating! And he's just a poor student, he's not some richy rich."

Dom scowled at him. "Oh, and you think that's where my viewpoint comes from?"

"No, I'm just saying—"

I turned, smirking, from eavesdropping on their conversation to Gus and Fitz, who sat on my end of the table.

Gus rolled his eyes, then cleared his throat and raised

his glass of wine—which he'd barely touched. He'd drink when we got back home. "Ahem. Attention, please."

The butlers grew quiet and shot Gus questioning looks. "I'd just like us all to toast to Minnie. She not only caught a killer but is also now officially back on the market!"

The guys all raised their glasses. "Cheers!"

"To Minnie."

Leo whistled.

Fitz lifted his glass of whiskey and gave me an earnest look. I clinked my flute of champagne against his glass, then turned to the rest of the table.

"Thank you, thank you!" My cheeks flushed hot. "And cheers to all of you. You're wonderful friends who had my back when I needed it most." I'd been really touched by the way they gathered around me to fend off Desmond.

"Aw." Cho waved me off. "You're making me blush."

I chuckled.

Dom nodded at me. "Anytime. We will be there."

As everyone finished their drinks, Fitz rose. "Next round is on me."

I pushed back from the table. "I'll go with you."

We hadn't really had a chance to talk yet, and I wanted to catch up with him. We threaded through crowded tables up to the bar and stood side by side, waiting to catch the busy bartender's attention.

Fitz leaned his elbows on the carved wood. "So... how're you feeling with all of this?" He looked down at me with concern. "The divorce being official, I mean."

I wrapped my fingers around the curved edge of the bar and drummed them. "Good, actually." I frowned. "A couple of months ago, I'd probably have had a good wallow about it. Pulled up old pictures and made myself miserable."

Fitz chuckled and looked down at his big hands.

I shrugged. "But life's a lot better now. I've got a job I love, great friends..." I darted a quick look at him. "You."

He looked up and our eyes met. I grinned and had to look away, my cheeks hot. I was saved from saying something even more awkward by the bartender sliding up in front of us.

"What'll you have?"

Fitz put in the order for the table, and the bartender moved off to make our drinks.

Fitz nodded. "Well, I'm glad to hear that life's looking up for you, Minnie."

I sighed. "It is. I'd still like to do a spell that'll get Desmond to leave me alone for good, but Mim told me I couldn't perform one until I had more closure." I quirked my lips to the side. "Ariel told me she felt closure with Petra, but it took her years and Petra's death to get it."

Fitz made a thoughtful noise.

"I don't think it'll take me that long." I grinned. "At least I hope not. But I think closure happens in stages, not necessarily all at once. But I feel more at peace with the divorce finalized. I think I'm heading in the right direction."

Fitz grinned down at me. "I agree."

"Oh! Speaking of spells." I lowered my voice and edged closer so my shoulder touched his cold arm. "Mim's going to teach me a protection spell I can put up around the tearoom and Gus's townhouse, if you're okay with it? It'll help keep you both safe from the vampire hunter."

Fitz fought a smile. "Thank you, Minnie. I'd be much obliged." He sucked in a deep breath, then blew it out. "So... what now? I'm sorry it didn't work out with the detective inspector."

I chuckled. "I'm not."

He looked at me, surprised.

I shrugged. "It was a good experience to get back out there in the dating game. And despite a murder, it wasn't as scary as I thought it would be."

Fitz hung his head. "I must confess, I admire your bravery."

I raised a brow at him. "Me? Brave?"

He nodded. "You are. It's been so long for me that approaching courting and love... it feels daunting. The whole world's so different now from the one I grew up in. I wouldn't know where to begin."

I chuckled, and he shot me a playful look. "And now you're laughing at me."

"No!" I placed my hand gently on his forearm. He stilled. "It's just... there might be dating apps now, and that sort of thing, but people are still just people, Fitz, and love's still love." I shrugged. "I think that's why Jane Austen's works are so enduringly popular. They're about many things, but chief among them, in my opinion, they're about love and relationships." I nudged him with my shoulder. "And that doesn't change all that much."

"Thank you."

I met his dark, intense eyes. "For what?"

"I've felt for so long, hundreds of years, like an outsider... out of place."

I frowned. "That must be so hard."

He gave me a small grin. "But you always make me feel at home."

My breath caught, and my mind went blank. How did he always manage to say the most touching things? And had he meant it romantically?

As I searched for something to say, he cleared his throat.

"Well, whether it's the detective or some other lucky man, I have no doubt you'll find love again, Minnie."

I chuckled. "It's definitely not going to be with Prescott. For one, he thinks I'm a clingy semi-stalker."

Fitz chuckled.

"And for another thing, he told me that he views supernatural creatures as monsters."

Fitz grunted. "That puts a bit of a damper on things."

I sighed. "With Desmond, I molded myself around him and his life and who he wanted me to be. I lived in his hometown, spent time with his friends, worked at his company. I kept big, important, magical parts of myself hidden for so long." I shook my head. "I won't do it again. I want to be working on myself, my writing, and learning to use my powers. When I get into another relationship, it'll be with someone who I can be my whole self around."

The bartender returned with our orders on a tray. "Just bring the tray back when you're done."

Fitz slid him payment and then plucked up my champagne flute and handed it to me. He lifted his glass of whiskey and met my eyes.

"I think what you just said is beautiful. To spending time with people who love you for yourself—your whole self."

I gulped and raised my glass to his. "Cheers, Fitz."

"Cheers, Minnie."

Think Minnie's magical adventures with Fitz and the tea room are over? No chance...

CLICK HERE to grab your copy of *English After-Doom Tea* so you can keep reading the Magical Tea Room Mysteries today!

AND MAKE sure you're on Erin's newsletter list, so you hear all about the monthly deals, giveaways, and new releases *and* get your exclusive magical mystery novella for FREE!

CLICK HERE to subscribe to Erin's Newsletter.

OTHER BOOKS BY ERIN JOHNSON

The Magical Tea Room Mysteries
Minnie Wells is working her marketing magic to save the coziest, vampire-owned tea room in Bath, England. But add in a string of murders, spells to learn, and a handsome Mr. Darcy-esque boss, and Minnie's cup runneth over with mischief and mayhem.

Spelling the Tea
With Scream and Sugar
A Score to Kettle
English After-Doom Tea

The Spells & Caramels Paranormal Cozy Mysteries
Imogen Banks is struggling to make it as a baker and a new witch on the mysterious and magical island of Bijou Mer. With a princely beau, a snarky baking flame and a baker's dozen of hilarious, misfit friends, she'll need all the help she can get when the murder mysteries start piling up.

Seashells, Spells & Caramels
Black Arts, Tarts & Gypsy Carts

Mermaid Fins, Winds & Rolling Pins
Cookie Dough, Snow & Wands Aglow
Full Moons, Dunes & Macaroons
Airships, Crypts & Chocolate Chips
Due East, Beasts & Campfire Feasts
Grimoires, Spas & Chocolate Straws
Eclairs, Scares & Haunted Home Repairs
Bat Wings, Rings & Apron Strings
* Christmas Short Story: Snowflakes, Cakes & Deadly Stakes

The Magic Market Paranormal Cozy Mysteries
A curse stole one witch's powers, but gave her the ability to speak with animals. Now Jolene helps a hunky police officer and his sassy, lie-detecting canine solve paranormal mysteries.

Pretty Little Fliers
Friday Night Bites
Game of Bones
Mouse of Cards
Pig Little Lies
Breaking Bat
The Squawking Dead
The Big Fang Theory

The Winter Witches of Holiday Haven
Running a funeral home in the world's most merry of cities has its downsides. For witch, Rudie Hollybrook, things can feel a little isolating. But when a murder rocks the festive town, Rudie's special skills might be the one thing that can help bring the killer to justice!

Cocoa Curses

Special Collections
The Spells & Caramels Boxset Books 1-3
Pet Psychic Mysteries Boxset Books 1-4
Pet Psychic Mysteries Boxset Books 5-8

Want to hang out with Erin and other magical mystery readers?

Come join Erin's VIP reader group on Facebook: **Erin's Bewitching Bevy.** It's a cauldron of fun!

GET YOUR FREE NOVELLA!

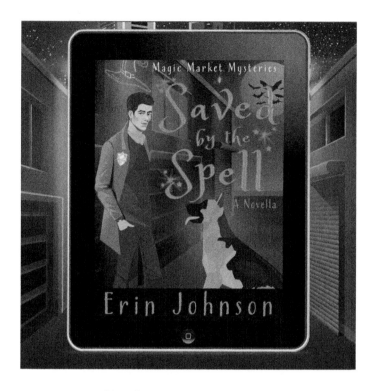

A magical academy. A suspicious death. Can an inexperienced cop expose the deadly secrets lurking behind bewitched classroom doors?

Download Saved by the Spell for FREE to solve a mystical murder today!

ABOUT THE AUTHOR

A native of Arizona, Erin loves her new home in the Pacific Northwest! She writes paranormal cozy mystery novels. These stories are mysterious, magical, and will hopefully make you laugh.

When not writing, she's hiking, napping with her dogs, and losing at trivia night.

You can find Erin at her website, **www. ErinJohnsonWrites.com** or on **Facebook.** Please email her at **erin@erinjohnsonwrites.com.** She loves to hear from readers!